Mystery Letters

Books by Beverly Lewis

GIRLS ONLY (GO!)
Youth Fiction

Dreams on Ice	*Follow the Dream*
Only the Best	*Better Than Best*
A Perfect Match	*Photo Perfect*
Reach for the Stars	*Star Status*

SUMMERHILL SECRETS
Youth Fiction

Whispers Down the Lane	*House of Secrets*
Secret in the Willows	*Echoes in the Wind*
Catch a Falling Star	*Hide Behind the Moon*
Night of the Fireflies	*Windows on the Hill*
A Cry in the Dark	*Shadows Beyond the Gate*

HOLLY'S HEART
Youth Fiction

Best Friend, Worst Enemy	*Straight-A Teacher*
Secret Summer Dreams	*No Guys Pact*
Sealed With a Kiss	*Little White Lies*
The Trouble With Weddings	*Freshman Frenzy*
California Crazy	*Mystery Letters*
Second-Best Friend	*Eight Is Enough*
Good-Bye, Dressel Hills	*It's a Girl Thing*

www.BeverlyLewis.com

Mystery Letters

BETHANYHOUSE

Minneapolis, Minnesota

Beverly Lewis

Cover design by Cheryl Neisen

Published by Bethany House Publishers
11400 Hampshire Avenue South
Bloomington, Minnesota 55438

Bethany House Publishers is a division of
Baker Publishing Group, Grand Rapids, Michigan.

Printed in the United States of America

ISBN-13: 978-0-7642-2619-9
ISBN-10: 0-7642-2619-3

Library of Congress Cataloging-in-Publication Data

Lewis, Beverly, 1949–
    Mystery letters / by Beverly Lewis. — [Rev., updated ed.]
        p.   cm. — (Holly's heart ; 12)
Summary: Holly is having a hard time with freshman algebra, and the
additional pressures of trying to figure out the identity of her secret admirer
and write the new advice column in the school paper almost make her forget
about Jesus.
    ISBN 0-7642-2619-3 (pbk.)
    [1. High schools—Fiction. 2. Schools—Fiction. 3. Letter writing—
Fiction. 4. Christian life—Fiction.] I. Title. II. Series: Lewis, Beverly,
1949-   . Holly's heart series ; 12.
PZ7L58464Myf   2003
[Fic]—dc21   2003001452

Author's Note

Several of my kid consultants were "on call" during the writing of this book and answered my questions whenever I asked. Thanks goes especially to Mindie Verplank, Larissa Paulson, Julie Buxman, Brandy Petty, Kelly Brinkley, and Amy Birch.

Dave Lewis, my husband and first editor, gave wise insight as always. Thanks to each of you—a fab-u-lous team!

To my HOLLY'S HEART fans
at Radiant Church:

Kelly Brinkley
Andrea Catalano
Jennifer Davis
Melissa Davis
Ali Drobeck
Megan Goerzen
Kris Harris
Beth Horner
Rachel Jones
Brittany Littleton
Tiffany Littleton
Tonya Nadeau
Amanda Neely

Cheryl Nelson
Colleen Nelson
Jennifer Noxon
Kimberly Noxon
Dani Root
Katie Root
Kim Stone
Tiffany Sturgeon
Stacy Tremble
Alicia Weckman
Brandi Weckman
Theresa Weckman

1

I hurried off the bus and rushed into the house. "Mom, I'm home!"

"Upstairs," she called back. "Mail's in the kitchen."

Grinning, I flung my jacket over a living room chair. Mom was mighty perceptive these days. Fact was, I'd been inquiring about the mail every day this week.

I made a beeline through the dining room to the corner of the kitchen, spying the letters on the desk. My fingers flicked through the stack. Bills, junk mail, letters . . .

Miss Holly Meredith caught my eye. I studied the familiar handwriting. Clear, even strokes. California—the return address.

Perfect. The letter I was waiting for! I held the cream-colored, textured envelope close to my heart. What had Sean Hamilton written *this* time?

Slowly, I turned the envelope over, starting to

open it. Then I noticed something strange. Scotch tape—two jagged pieces—stuck to the back of the envelope. Hmm. I'd been getting letters from Sean nearly every week—emails, too—since school started, and he *never* used tape to seal the envelope.

"Mom!"

"Don't yell, I'm right here," she said, coming into the kitchen.

"Where's Carrie?" I demanded.

Her blue eyes squinted almost shut. "Holly, please don't start something with your sister."

I showed her the envelope. "There's only one person in the house who'd do this."

Mom sat on a stool and leaned her elbows heavily on the island bar. "Be careful about accusing someone, Holly-Heart." She sighed. "Carrie might not have anything to do with it."

"And she might have *everything* to do with it!" I stormed out of the kitchen and down the steps to the family room, clutching the envelope. Carrie-the-Snoop, just turned ten, sat on the floor watching TV. Stephie, our eight-year-old stepsister and cousin (because Uncle Jack married Mom after his first wife—our aunt—died) lounged on the sectional. Both sets of eyes were totally focused on the tube.

"Okay, you two, listen up," I said. Neither of them paid attention, so I stood in front of Carrie, waving the envelope in her face.

"Hey, you're blocking my view," she hollered.

"I'll move when you explain this." I pointed to the tape on the back of the envelope.

Her mouth curled into a surly smile. "Yeah, so? I

read your letter. Who cares?"

"Mom!" I dashed upstairs to the kitchen, hoping she was still there. She wasn't. Goofey, my cat, glanced up at me from his sunny square on the floor. A brown patch of fur colored the gray around one eye. I leaned down and stroked his motley fur. "My sister's a total nightmare," I complained.

Goofey agreed and gave a comforting *me-e-o-ow*.

I stood up and headed for the doorway leading to the lower level. "Okay for you, Carrie. You'll be sorry, I promise."

"See if I care. You're wasting time. Go read your love letter from Sean."

Love letter? I gulped. She must've read through the whole letter. Sean never started his letters out mushy, but sometimes at the end . . .

I fumed. How could she do this? Just when I hoped things were improving between Carrie and me. I mean, she was a preteen now. Man, if this was how life with Carrie was going to be at ten, I hated to think about her full-blown teen years!

I turned and ran two floors up to the master bedroom at the end of the hall. The door was cracked slightly. "Mom?" I whispered, trying to control my rage. At one point, both she and Uncle Jack had promised stiffer laws for snoopers. Stuff like no TV for a full week. And double kitchen duty. Threats of that sort of discipline being dished out did seem to help some. But not much.

I peeked around the door to see Mom sacked out on the bed. Her face looked pale and her eyes were a bit puffy. Was she sick?

Without disturbing her, I left the room, closing the door silently behind me. Goofey was right under my feet; I nearly tripped over him. Picking him up, I pressed my face into the back of his neck and tiptoed to my room. There, I settled down on my window seat, still holding Goofey close. He didn't protest, but when I began to open Sean's letter, Goofey slinked off my lap and sat opposite me on the padded seat, eyes glaring.

"Don't be silly," I laughed. "It's not really a love letter." I opened the envelope and began to read.

2

October 7
Dear Holly,

As always, I enjoyed your letter. Thanks for writing back so quickly. It was interesting to hear that, as the new assistant editor for your school paper, you'll be writing your own column. My friends and I think The Summit is a cool name for a high-school paper in a Colorado mountain town. So . . . when's your first column scheduled to appear? I definitely want a copy of my Holly's creative literary work—in print.

I stopped reading.

My Holly? Had I read correctly? I scanned the line again. Yep!

I remembered Carrie's nasty smile and flippant response to my reprimand. *Oh, great. She knows about this, too!*

It took more than the usual amount of self-control to keep myself from charging downstairs and wringing her little neck. My reward for staying put—

not giving in to temptation—came as the delicious autumn sun warmed my shoulders. I let myself lean back against the window on my multi-pillowed seat, savoring Sean's words.

His letter turned out to be shorter than usual. I finished reading it in a few minutes, only to reread the first several paragraphs again. Sean seemed sincerely interested in my new editorial position on the school paper. He was the kind of guy most girls would give their eyeteeth for.

If only Carrie would keep her nose out!

♥   ♥   ♥

Mom rested until Uncle Jack arrived home. I heard his footsteps on the stairs, and he headed straight for their bedroom. It was all I could do to keep from poking my head into the hall and eavesdropping. Mom seemed awfully tired lately. I hoped she wasn't coming down with a case of the fall flu.

Around here, the change of seasons wreaked havoc with us locals. The first snowfall always brought out-of-town tourists and ski bums, some from overseas. And with the start of the ski season came a variety of international flu bugs. Fortunately, I hadn't succumbed to any of them yet.

A few minutes passed, and I was aware of Uncle Jack hurriedly leaving the house with Stan, Phil, and Mark, my three brousins—cousins-turned-stepbrothers. Something was up.

In less than thirty minutes, they returned with pizza and soda for everyone. I guess Mom wasn't well enough to cook supper. She was even too sick to come down and sit at the table with us. Rats! I needed her input tonight when I brought up Carrie's snooping violation.

Not-so-patiently I waited until after Uncle Jack's prayer. Carrie eyeballed me, looking profoundly sheepish. It was time.

"Uncle Jack," I began. "I thought you should know . . . Carrie opened my mail today."

My stepdad's slice of pizza halted midway between his plate and his mouth. His eyes shifted to Carrie, several place settings away. "I thought we had this problem worked out months ago."

I spoke up. "And that's not all. She's acting all hotsy-totsy about it, too." I felt like a tattling third grader instead of a freshman in high school.

"Have you forgotten the consequences for this kind of behavior?" he asked, still gazing at Carrie.

Yes!

"I . . . uh . . ." Carrie sputtered.

"You must never open someone else's mail—snail mail or email," he continued. "Including your older sister's."

Carrie acted cool about the reprimand, but her cocky attitude was squelched quickly when the sentencing came.

"No TV or phone privileges for a week," Uncle Jack stated. "Starting tonight."

"No phone?" she wailed.

Uncle Jack resumed eating his pizza. When he'd

chewed and swallowed, he took a long drink of soda. "Now"—and here, he leaned forward slightly—"your mother is resting quietly, Carrie, so don't get any ideas about going to her with your whining."

I'd never heard Uncle Jack come down so hard on Carrie, or on anyone, for that matter. Something was definitely bothering him. And I was fairly sure it had nothing to do with Carrie's snooping.

"Is Mom sick?" I ventured.

"She's going to need a good amount of rest," he said guardedly.

"Can I go up and see her?" Stephie asked.

Uncle Jack nodded. "Later, when she wakes up."

Stephie's eyes filled with tears. "Is *this* mommy gonna die, too?"

Uncle Jack pushed his chair back and went to his youngest daughter. "Mommy's not that sick," he reassured her.

Phil, eleven, and Mark, nine, looked concerned as their dad hoisted Stephie up and out of her chair and carried her into the living room. The rest of us tried not to watch. Stephie, after all, was the baby of the family. Possibly Uncle Jack's favorite, if such a thing could be. She was the image of her deceased mother, my aunt Marla, who had been my all-time favorite relative.

I tried to ignore the hard lump in my throat. And the strange, fluttery feeling in my stomach—a confusing mixture of hunger and worry. We all ate in silence while Stephie sniffled in the living room in Uncle Jack's arms.

Finally, after we finished pigging out, Stan, the

oldest of the Meredith-Patterson clan, suggested we clear the table.

"But it's not my turn," Carrie insisted.

"C'mon, Carrie," I said. "Stop fussing and help."

"You stay out of it!" she shot back.

Stan grabbed her arm and guided her gingerly out to the kitchen. "Look, little girl, do I have to *make* you wanna help?"

"I'm not little," she wailed. "And I'm telling." She made a face. "Uncle Jack!"

Mark cupped his hand over her mouth. "Didn't you hear what Dad just said about letting Mom rest?"

"He's *your* dad, not mine!" With that, she pulled away from both Stan and Mark, plowed through the dining room, and nearly knocked a pile of paper plates out of Phil's hands.

That was my cue to exit the kitchen. I'd had it with Carrie's lousy attitude. What my flesh-and-blood sister needed was a good heart-to-heart talk. Starting with her ridiculous notion about Uncle Jack's place in our family.

3

I didn't bother to knock—I barged right into Carrie's room. Determined, I closed the door behind me. "We have to talk."

"Says who?" she sneered.

I sat down on her bed, praying silently for the right words. "Look, I know you're mad at me because of the letter."

"You're dangy-dong right I am. You didn't have to go and tell on me."

"That's true; I didn't," I replied softly. "But you can't seem to conquer your snooping addiction. What kind of big sister would I be if I didn't intervene?"

She crossed her arms over her chest and exhaled loudly. "Stop talking so grown-up, Holly. You think you're such a big shot because you're in high school. Well, I'll tell you what kind of sister you really are."

"Carrie, keep your voice down."

She screwed up her face. "I wish you'd just go

away and leave me alone."

We sat there, staring at each other. Finally I turned away, facing her bulletin board. A small black-and-white picture of our dad was stuck on the board with a white thumbtack. He'd autographed it for her last Christmas when we'd gone to California for a visit. *Robert Meredith*, the scribbled letters ran across the bottom.

"What are you staring at?" Carrie demanded.

I turned to her. "You're angry at Daddy, aren't you?"

"Why shouldn't I be?" she spouted. "He left us, didn't he? Went off to California without us. Divorced Mom. Left us kids behind." The tears spilled down her face. "All those years he belonged here."

I understood her pain. Oh, how I knew . . .

Yet I'd dealt with it—worked things out with myself about the divorce. With God's help. Daddy's, too. But I knew exactly how Carrie was feeling. The whole Daddy thing had started for me several years ago. The questioning . . . the wondering . . . those wretched feelings of worthlessness . . . the rejection.

And now, as I looked into Carrie's face, I could see the hideous thing already rearing its head in my preadolescent sister. "Carrie," I whispered, reaching for her hand. "Let me tell you about Daddy . . . and Mom."

Carrie listened through a veil of tears and occasional sobs. It surprised me that she was experiencing this stuff now. Lots of young girls experienced the emotional ups and downs of the prepuberty roller coaster. For some, it started at age nine. Shoot, I'd worried myself nearly sick in seventh grade wondering when I'd ever become a "real" woman. And now here I was, helping my little sister cope with what appeared to be a full-blown hormonal upheaval.

"It's not your fault about the divorce," I explained gently. Mom had told me the same thing when I was twelve. "Our parents weren't Christians back then. Things were a little crazy, from what Mom says. She wasn't as submissive as Daddy thought she should be, and Daddy had his heart set on a career instead of his family."

"How'd you find out all this stuff?" she asked.

"Little bits at a time. Every so often I'd sit Mom down and ask her questions. And after my second visit to California at Christmas, I started to feel more comfortable with Daddy."

She pouted, looking down at the floor. "He likes you best."

"Why do you think that?"

"I just do."

"Well, I can tell you one thing. Daddy really wanted you to come along last summer. Remember when Andie and I flew out there together? He was really disappointed."

Her face brightened a bit. "Are you sure?"

"Perfectly sure."

She stood up and walked over to the bulletin board. "I wish I knew him better."

"Maybe you will someday. But till then, be thankful that he's become a Christian. Oh, and something else." I paused, studying the girl who was a miniature me. "Please try to be thankful about Uncle Jack."

She shrugged.

"C'mon, Carrie, you know how wonderful he is to Mom. Honestly, he's the best thing that could've happened to this poor, messed-up family."

"But . . . he's only a stepdad," she insisted.

"Only? He's the *best* stepdad ever."

Carrie looked at me, startled. "You really think so?"

"Give him a chance. You'll see."

She wrinkled her nose. "That's easy for you to say. You're not on restriction."

"It's only a week. Besides, you can't blame Uncle Jack for that."

She pulled on her long blond ponytail. "A week without the phone is an eternity."

"You'll survive." I got up and gave her a hug. The anger between us had pretty much fizzled. "Still friends?"

"Do I have a choice?" She twirled her ponytail around her finger, the way I used to when I was little. I headed for the hall.

Back in my room, I sorted through a zillion homework papers, especially the miserable algebra assignment for the weekend. I couldn't stop thinking of Sean's letter and his astonishing words. Thank goodness Carrie hadn't mentioned anything in her usual snippy manner. More than anything, I hoped she'd keep the romantic angle quiet from Mom.

Poor Mom. She'd spent the whole afternoon and

now the evening in her room. Did I dare peek in?

I muddled through my math homework, carelessly going from one insignificant set of problems to another. What good would algebra do me in the future? I wanted to be a writer, for pete's sake!

Thirty minutes passed while I fussed over a mere two problems.

The phone rang. Stan yelled up the stairs, "Holly, it's Andie."

"I'll get it up here." I wondered how I could talk on the hall phone but keep my comments from floating down the hall to Mom's ears. That is, if she was awake.

"Hey, girl," Andie said when I answered. "I'm writing a letter to the assistant editor of *The Summit*." She laughed into the phone. "That's you, remember?"

"What's going on?"

"Just wanted to keep you on your editorial toes, you know. Wanted to come up with a really off-the-wall letter for you to answer in your new column."

It was my turn to laugh. "Look, I'm not playing Dr. Laura, if that's what you think."

"Have you thought up a cool name for your column yet?" she asked.

"At the moment I'm trying to think up some cool answers for my rotten algebra homework."

"On a Friday night—are you nuts?"

"Why not?"

Andie snickered. "Join the ranks of the procrastinators of the world. Wait till late *Sunday* night."

"Not me; I'd flunk for sure." We talked about *The*

Summit some more and then how glad she was about not taking a foreign language. "I think you're making a big mistake," I said. "French class is fabulous."

"If you say so." I could hear her whispering in the background.

"Who're you talking to?" I asked.

"Somebody wants to know if you'll go out with him," she said, trying to keep from laughing.

"Andie, this is *so* junior high. C'mon!"

"Just answer one question. Are you tied up with anyone right now?"

"Uh, not really."

"What about Sean?" she asked. "You two still writing?"

The way she said it made me wonder if she was hoping I'd say no. "Uh, this is a little personal, don'tcha think?"

More whispering.

"Andie, who are you talking to? Who's over there?"

Loud, hilarious laughter. Andie's . . . and some guy's.

"Andie, talk to me," I demanded.

Several more seconds of stupidity passed. Finally I couldn't stand it anymore and hung up.

Funniest thing. I didn't care two hoots about the guy at Andie's house inquiring about me. Nope, didn't care one bit. Sean Hamilton and I were very good friends. And that's all that mattered to me.

I slammed my algebra book shut and went down the hall.

Mom was awake and in the master bathroom. I could see the light coming from the crack under the door as I peeked around her antique pine dresser. The faucet was on and swishing sounds came from the sink. She was either washing her face or brushing her teeth. A good sign.

I decided not to wait around for her, and I headed downstairs to make a cup of cocoa. Phil and Stephie showed up just as I plopped a handful of miniature marshmallows in my hot chocolate.

"Where's mine?" Phil sniffed the sweet aroma.

I pushed his head away from my after-supper treat. "You're not helpless." I pointed toward the mug tree on the kitchen counter. "Make your own."

Stephie muttered something and ran back downstairs to join Uncle Jack and the remaining family members. Phil, however, hung around acting like he wanted to talk. He sat at the bar, still eyeing my cup of cocoa. "Was seventh grade cool?" Phil asked.

I smiled. "Not as cool as ninth."

"So . . . what's it like, in your opinion?"

I stirred the marshmallows, watching them melt into foamy white suds. "You've got a whole school year to worry about it."

"Maybe not." He scratched his head. "The counselor gave me another test today."

"What kind of test?"

"Just an assessment test to see if I'm too smart for my britches, like Mom says."

I smirked at his comment. "So your teachers must think you're gifted or something."

He nodded enthusiastically. "You're lookin' at the first eleven-year-old genius at Dressel Hills Middle School. I'll be skipping a grade soon—going into the seventh-grade TAG program."

"Talented and gifted—you?" This was the first I'd heard this.

Phil got up and swaggered around the kitchen. He grabbed a cup off the mug tree and turned on the faucet, gloating all the while. "Betcha can't guess what my best subject is?" He shot me an impish grin. "Actually, I'm brilliant in all subjects, but, hey, I wouldn't be surprised if they hired me out as a tutor in—"

"Spare me," I groaned. I'd had enough of his crowing and strutting. Especially after I'd struggled away my entire Friday night on homework.

"Give up?" he taunted.

I shrugged uncaringly.

"Math. I'm a marvel," he exclaimed. "Algebra, geometry, you name it."

I nearly choked at his arrogance, not to mention the frustration over my own recent algebraic nightmare. "Pride goes before destruction . . ." I said, quoting the proverb.

Phil opened his mouth for a comeback, but Mom came into the kitchen just then. She looked rested, refreshed. "Where *is* everyone?" she asked.

"Downstairs in the family room." I slid off the bar stool and went to her. "Feeling better, Mom?"

She nodded, returning my hug. "Much better."

"Do you want some peppermint tea with honey?" I asked. "I'll make it for you."

"Sounds good, thanks." She sat down at the bar as I slid Phil's cup of cocoa out of the microwave to make room.

"I can see who rates around here," Phil said to Mom. "Holly wouldn't cook for *me*."

I suppressed a laugh. "You'll get over it."

Mom ignored our bantering and smoothed her blond hair. "Well, Phil," she said, "I've been hearing some terrific things about you."

Yeah, yeah, I thought. *Do we have to rehash this?*

Phil was all too happy to give her the rundown on his latest test scores and teacher remarks. I stirred the honey into Mom's cup and quietly exited the room. It was time to answer someone's letter—someone very special. Whether Andie liked it or not.

♥   ♥   ♥

Normally Jared Wilkins and Amy-Liz Thompson (his latest girlfriend) sat toward the back of the classroom and off to one side in algebra. Always together. Today they sat on opposite sides of the room. I gave their present classroom positions only a fleeting thought, then tore into my notebook, hunting down the pathetic homework I'd toiled and fretted over during my entire weekend.

Andie Martinez slid into the desk behind me. "Did you get your homework done?"

"I guess you could call it done. Did you?"

"Late last night," she admitted. "Couldn't let it spoil my weekend, you know." I remembered her comment about procrastinators. She'd practiced what she preached.

Billy Hill hurried in, grabbed a seat across from Andie, and took out a pencil. Andie leaned over and whispered something to him. I could hear their voices buzzing behind me.

A few seconds later Mrs. Franklin, our resident math wizard, made her debut. Andie kept whispering with Billy, but I ignored them. Mrs. Franklin was getting her things situated and I watched intently, scrutinizing her every move. What sort of woman— a married, civilized woman—would want to teach high-school algebra? What motivated her to impose nightmarish assignments on students? And for money no less?

I tore out a sheet of lined paper and jotted down some of her obvious characteristics. Who knows— this true-to-life description might fit into one of my stories. Or maybe even my editorial column some-day.

Mrs. Franklin

1. Too aloof
2. Pinched up in the face (from creating too many excruciating math problems?)
3. No jewelry—not even a wedding band (is she Amish?)
4. No makeup (sure could use some!)

I ran my hand through my hair, eager to turn in my homework and have the worst hour of the entire day behind me. Third hour . . . forty-five agonizing minutes to go.

At the risk of drawing attention to myself, I began gathering up homework papers from students in my row. Jared grinned when I glanced his way. "That's it, take charge, Holly-Heart," he said.

His comment didn't strike me as odd at the time. He'd never been one to comment publicly on things or call me by my nickname in front of other students, at least not in high school, but I thought he was just flirting. It was second nature with him. As much a part of his personality as my compulsion to write.

I collected several more students' papers, then headed down the opposite row. When I came to Billy's desk, he handed his homework to me. Funny thing, though. His face blotched red, and he glanced away.

I'd never known Billy to be shy around me. We'd become friends back in seventh grade when he helped me set up certain things (and people) at my thirteenth birthday party. Later, he started showing up at youth activities with Danny Myers, another friend, at my church.

Billy and I were just good friends. There was nothing else between us. Nothing. Andie, however, had another spin on the subject. And she told me so while I stashed my books in my locker after algebra. "Billy's crazy about you."

"He's what?"

Andie grinned, leaning back against the lockers. "He wants to know if you'll go out with him."

I was dumbfounded. "How do you know?"

"He was at my house Friday night," she confessed. "He made me call you."

"Billy did?"

She grinned. "Isn't it cool?"

"What's Paula Miller think? I mean, isn't she going out with Billy?"

She waved her hand. "It's October—we're well into the school year. People start looking around, getting antsy about now."

"Oh, I get it. You're trying to talk me into this Billy thing, right?" I closed my locker door and pressed the combination lock in place.

"Not exactly." She tossed her dark curls and looked away. Billy was coming down the hall. His face turned radish-red when he spotted me with Andie. Having a crush on someone changes your complete outlook—good friends or not.

"Look, Andie, I don't want to hurt anyone," I

whispered. "But I'm not interested in anything more than friendship."

She turned quickly, looking at me with penetrating brown eyes. "Will you listen? Billy's not just any guy."

"Don't you think *I* know that? He and I—we're friends. I'd just like to keep it that way."

She followed me to the cafeteria, and after we went through the hot-lunch line and found a table, the conversation got started all over again. "Open your eyes," Andie said, gazing around at the crowd of kids chowing down. "There are new guy horizons everywhere you look. Take your pick."

I wondered what warped romance novel she'd been reading. "Get a life." I reached for my milk carton.

She sighed. "I'm *living* in the real world. You . . . you're hiding out with your fantasies."

"Excuse me?"

"Letter-writing is a total waste. Sean Hamilton can't take the place of a real, live guy."

I scoffed. "That's what you think. You just don't know Sean well enough. He's far better than any of the guys around here."

"Thank goodness for that."

"Andie, that's rude, really rude."

She stopped eating. "And so are you . . . turning Billy down like this." And with that she got up, leaving her tray behind.

"Finally, peace and quiet," I mumbled to myself, wondering what the hype about a flesh-and-blood guy was all about. Andie was the one who needed to wake up to reality.

Me? I was perfectly content to live in my—how did she put it?—"fantasy world." It sure beat the stupidity of playing musical chairs, high-school style.

5

After school I went to see Marcia Greene, student editor for *The Summit*. Her brother, Zye, the senior class president, and his sidekick, Ryan Davis, were hanging around outside the door. I avoided eye contact with the two of them. Freshman initiation was still too fresh in my memory!

"Hey, Holly," Ryan said, following me into the classroom. "Had anything new published?"

"Nope."

"Aren't you working on some big novel or something?" He was pushing, and I was mad.

"You don't know what you're talking about." It was my stall tactic. I was working on an outline for a mini-novel, but it was certainly none of his beeswax.

Ever since I'd met Ryan Davis last summer, I found him to be repulsive. Plainly put, he bugged me. Maybe it was because he kept asking about my one and only published piece, "Love Times Two," like I was some celebrity or something. I'd sold the short story to a teen magazine last year. Pure luck . . . and a lot of hard work.

Actually, Stan had been the one to spill the beans about my only by-line, because Ryan was also interested in getting published. But from my perspective, Ryan Davis didn't seem like the literary type. Writers were people who needed to be racially accepting—completely unbiased. Ryan, however, was prejudiced. And I resented that about him.

"So . . . nothing new?" he continued. "What about that new column of yours? That counts, doesn't it?"

I didn't exactly want to stand here talking to this known jerk about my most recent link with the school paper. He was fishing for personal info, and I felt uncomfortable. Quickly, I went to talk to Marcia. Out of the corner of my eye, I noticed Ryan leave with Zye. Good, now I could relax.

Marcia's desk was piled with papers and what looked like art roughs from students. She glanced up from her work, eyes shining. "Glad you came, Holly. Mrs. Ross gave me the go-ahead to approve some last-minute changes."

Mrs. Ross, formerly Miss W, was now my high-school English teacher. The good-natured woman was also in charge of overseeing the school paper. Because she had always been my favorite teacher in junior high, I was thrilled that she'd opted to teach high-school English this year.

I pulled up a chair, peering at Marcia's desk. "What's our deadline? Are we running behind?"

"Actually, pretty close to schedule." She glanced at the calendar. "Today's Monday the fourteenth. Less than ten days before this mess goes to the printer." She pushed her glasses up and studied me. "Can you get your column to me by next Monday?"

"Sure. But I haven't thought of a name for it yet."

"No problem." She stuck her pencil behind one ear. "We can brainstorm tomorrow—first thing if you like. Oh, by the way, your box is crammed with letters." She pointed to a wall of wooden cubicles, which were the mailboxes for appointed personnel. One had my name on it.

Quickly, I abandoned my notebook and books on the chair and went to investigate. Marcia was right. There were lots of letters. Several with familiar handwriting—Andie's, for one. "I'll sort through these tonight," I said.

"Be sure and check out the back of that long business envelope," Marcia said, smiling.

I found the envelope she was referring to and observed the weird acrostic on the back. It spelled out the five journalistic Ws—who, what, when, where, and why. "What's this about?"

"Guess you'll have to read the contents. Let me know if it seems to be from anyone interesting."

"Yeah, right. Interesting . . ." I thought of Sean just then. There was only one *really* interesting person on the face of the earth. At least for me.

Reaching for my notebook, I opened it to the section marked *The Summit*. When I did, my assignment from algebra floated out. I leaned down under the chair and reached for it. I'd written Mrs. Frank-lin's name in the upper left-hand corner. Hmm ... How and when could I incorporate the perfect description I'd written of her into my column?

I found the algebra section of my notebook and secured the boring assignment, hunting for the wacky description of the salaried math wizard—the list I'd written during third period.

Checking through several homework pages and quizzes, I found nothing. I frowned. Where was it?

I searched through my algebra book. Surely I'd put it inside the book, safe from nosy eyes. But no, not there, either.

Worry bit at my thoughts. Had the paper gotten mixed in with student homework papers? I remembered gathering them up, row by row. Trying to be helpful in that class was all I could offer. Alas, trying to actually do algebra was getting me absolutely nowhere.

I exited the student newspaper office and dashed through the hall to the algebra classroom where I suffered daily. Slowly I peeked inside. The teacher's desk was vacant. Perfect!

Without breathing, I hurried into the room and glanced around, making sure no one was hiding under a desk. I flipped through a few papers on the top of the long, wide desk. Cautiously, I opened the top right drawer. Inside I found a group of test papers. Unfortunately, they were for students in fourth hour.

My heart sank. I closed the drawer and left.

"Where *is* that paper?" I mumbled to myself all the way to my locker.

Danny Myers waved to me in the hall, but I barely saw him.

Amy-Liz flagged me down. "Hey, are you in a trance?"

"Huh?"

"Holly? You okay?" She frowned.

"Not really."

"What's wrong?" She walked with me to my locker.

"I'll let you know tomorrow after third hour."

She held on to my locker door, leaning close. "Look, if you ever need to . . . uh, want to talk, about a guy, well, I'm here."

I was stunned. Where was *this* coming from? "What guy?"

"Holly, it's okay. I know what's going on with Billy," she whispered, touching my arm. "And believe me, I think I know what you're going through."

"You do?" I eeked out. I probably sounded totally dense, and at the moment, I felt that way, too. Here she was going on about guys and the misery thereof, and I was worried about my academic future.

When I got home, I didn't even bother calling Andie to find out what Amy-Liz meant by "what's going on with Billy?" It was absolutely pointless. Besides, Amy-Liz had no idea that Billy had asked Andie to ask me out. Did she?

Of course, guy-news always traveled fast. At least in small ski towns like Dressel Hills. People talked about what they heard. That's just how it was.

So maybe Amy-Liz *had* heard something. That I'd turned Billy Hill down via Andie the self-appointed mediator. If only Billy had approached me himself. I could've leveled with him gently. But, of course, guys never did sensible things like that. Setting up someone indirectly was how the guy-girl thing worked around here.

At supper Mom and Uncle Jack lauded Phil's amazing test scores. In fact, the entire meal was filled with talk of my younger brousin. I couldn't wait for it to end.

"Just think," Stephie spouted, "our brother's a genius."

"Sure as shootin'," Uncle Jack replied, looking proud.

Then and there I came to the realization that I could never bring myself to ask my parents for help with homework. Not as long as Phil's accomplishments took center stage. Some might call it jealousy, but I knew the truth. Sibling rivalry didn't set well with me. Especially when the sibling was younger.

After kitchen cleanup, I settled down to another evening alone in my room, wracking my brain. More algebra homework. Not just one page—three! I thought I'd die. Die and never be fully appreciated for the good effort I'd made—trying to keep my proverbial head above water. But no. I was sinking fast. And six-week deficiency reports were coming out in four days—Friday.

I slept very little that night. And when sleep did come, it was accompanied by fragmented dreams. Either I or someone close to me was searching for a paper. Searching frantically, and not finding it.

Once when I'd awakened, too frazzled to go back to sleep, I remembered the strange envelope with the five Ws listed on the back. I was wobbly, but I managed to turn on the light beside my bed, drag myself out of the covers, and walk the length of my room. On my desk, I found my backpack and rummaged through till I found the stack of letters.

I carried the weird one back to bed with me. There, in the wee hours, I opened the long, thin envelope.

Dear Holly,

You must be aware of the journalistic "5 Ws," right? Well, I would like to begin with the first W— that's WHO, in case you forgot. So . . . WHO are you really? Oh yeah, I know your name. But WHAT about the nickname, Holly-Heart? WHO gave you such a nickname and WHAT does it mean? WHEN can I expect your answer? And WHERE will the answer be in your column? (Top and center, lower middle, or heaven forbid . . . the tail end.) You choose.

Oh yes. Certainly there must be a reason WHY such an unusual nickname. I will await your reply.

Signed—WHO am I?

"Why me?" I gasped. Laughing, I fell back into my pillows. The letter was just what I needed to get my mind off the lost paper. I fell into a deep sleep, without a single dream.

♥   ♥   ♥

Mrs. Too-aloof-pinched-faced-Franklin did a number on me the next day when she passed back our homework. Mine looked like it was bleeding. Zillions of red ink marks were all over and . . .

Gasp!

Something was stapled to the last page. My list! And there was a note on it in the teacher's own hand. *Please see me after class today.*

Gulp!

Only one sane thought grabbed me: *Help me, dear Lord.*

All through class—fifty minutes of fear—I trembled. And when it came time for the bell, I remained at my desk, waiting for everyone to clear out. It took forever, though, because some kid kept hanging around asking Mrs. Franklin idiotic questions. Stuff even *I* knew the answers to. And algebraically speaking, that was saying a lot.

Finally he left, and my teacher sat at her desk. I figured it was my cue to stand up and walk up there—to hear the words I'd feared the most. That she had no choice but to fail me outright. I'd scoffed and scorned her very personage. I'd described her to a T. . . .

"Holly," she began, "about your grade . . ."

Here it comes, I thought. *I'm doomed.*

"Is there something I might do to help you?" she asked.

I nearly choked. "Something?" I whispered.

She nodded. "What is there about algebra you don't understand?"

"Everything," I admitted. "Absolutely everything."

She tapped her unpolished nails on the desk. "I see. And are you paying attention in class?"

Here we go, I thought. *Now comes the lecture about writing descriptive lists instead of listening.*

She waited silently.

I took a deep breath. "Uh . . . I try to pay attention, but not much of it makes sense." I waited for her reply and to be cast out.

"Are you college-bound?" she asked unexpectedly.

"I hope so."

Her face suddenly pinched up tighter than before. "And what is it you hope to embrace as your major field of study?"

"English and journalism." I felt my knees shaking. What might she do with this information? Have me kicked off the school paper, perhaps? Mrs. Ross would be heartbroken, and so would I.

"Then you'll be needing to acquire a passing grade in my class, is that correct?" she said with finality. The conversation was coming to a close. Hallelujah.

"Yes, ma'am," I said. "And do you have any suggestions as to how I might do that?" I nearly choked on my own words. Shoot, I was starting to sound just like her.

"A tutor would be in order," came her reply. She rustled through a small black notebook on her desk. "I may have just the person for you."

I wondered who on earth could knock algebraic sense into this poor mass of intellect I called my brain. Who?

"Here we are," she said. "Jot down this number: 555-4323."

"Uh, excuse me, Mrs. Franklin, but that's *my* number!"

She picked up her notebook again, studying it. "Well, there must be some mistake. I don't quite understand."

She surveyed me with a forced smile that added

to the severity of her face. "Your legal last name is Meredith, correct?"

I had no idea what she was getting at. "Yes, ma'am."

"Well, then, this is very strange. The name given here is a Philip Patterson."

No! I nearly shouted the word. Instead, I clutched my throat. Not Phil, my disgustingly smart little brousin. Not him!

Mrs. Franklin looked up. "Is there a problem?"

"Uh . . . no, not really, er . . . yes, I believe there must be some mistake. You see, that name—the name you just said—happens to be my eleven-year-old stepbrother."

"Oh, I see." The slightest twinge of a smile threatened to crease her wrinkled face. Threatened to reveal the truth. Some might call it poetic justice—after what I'd written about her. I couldn't help but think as I left the classroom that Mrs. Franklin was probably having a hard time keeping her stern face straight about now.

I gathered up my things and headed to my locker . . . in a fog. How had Phil's name shown up on Mrs. Franklin's tutoring list? How? I thought back to the conversation last night at supper. I had tuned out much of it on purpose. Why? Because I was sick of the hoopla at home over Phil. And now this. What could I do? There was no way on earth I'd succumb to having my stepbrother tutor me. *Pas mon frère!*

I decided to work harder. Maybe even twist Andie's arm about helping me. Anything else would be better. That's when I spotted Billy. He'd seen me and made his usual attempt at glancing away, almost shyly. So weird for a guy who used to be able to talk to me about anything.

I thought about going over and discussing my algebra dilemma. But, no, that wouldn't be fair. Besides, he might get the wrong idea.

"Holly," a voice called to me.

I turned around to see Andie flying down the hall. I expected her to stop and talk and go to lunch with me. "Hey, where're you going?" I asked.

"Got to warn Jared about tomorrow," she said. "Didja hear about a pop quiz in algebra?"

Yikes! "Tomorrow?"

"Yeah, Franklin told her second hour about it but forgot to tell us. So I assume it'll be a major surprise."

I groaned. "Oh, great, just what I *don't* need."

"What? Are you still having trouble?"

"You could say that. Want to help me?"

Andie burst out laughing. "Do I look like I can explain X plus the unknown factor equals Y? Do I?"

"But what about the quiz? What's it on?" I pleaded.

"Beats me, but it's going to count as one-third of our grade. I heard that for sure."

Help, somebody help!

"What's Jared doing today after school?" I asked.

She shook her head. "No way, huh-uh! You're not linking up with him."

"But if he can make heads and tails out of it for

me, why not? I mean, it's not like we'd be together or anything."

Andie's eyes grew serious. "Jared's vulnerable right now. Read my lips. He's been dumped—ego bruised."

"By Amy-Liz?"

Andie nodded. "None other than."

"Whoa, Charlie!" Amazing news.

"I know. It does take courage—as you know."

"All too well." I closed my locker. "Well, guess I'm winging it. Shoot, I can't decide what I should do first—pray or study."

"Try both," Andie said with a wave and a grin.

"Yeah." I headed for the cafeteria alone.

7

While standing in the hot-lunch line, I spotted Marcia Greene. She saw me, too. "Holly, I thought you were dropping by *The Summit* office this morning."

I'd forgotten. "Oh, sorry. Uh, I had this thing in algebra."

"Can we talk during lunch?" she asked. "Maybe we can come up with a title for your column."

"Yeah, maybe. Sometimes when you're doing something else—like eating—ideas come more easily." While we ate hot dogs and chili, we brainstormed. Jared and Danny came over and helped. Billy, too; rather reticently, however. Jared must've noticed the change in Billy's demeanor because there was a surprising surge of unspoken interest directed toward me. Jared was the all-time master flirt. I almost felt sorry for Billy, just trying to cope— to be himself around me.

Jared spoke up, "The best column titles so far are

these: 'In Beat With Holly-Heart,' 'Holly Speaks Out,' and 'Dear Holly.' "

"I like 'In Beat With Holly-Heart.' What do you think?" Marcia asked me.

I remembered the anonymous letter querying me about my nickname. "Maybe I should leave off my nickname."

"But why?" Jared said. "It's so . . . you."

Billy nodded. "Everyone calls you Holly-Heart."

"They do?" This was news to me.

"The guys do, right?" Marcia asked Jared.

"Maybe not to Holly's face, but yeah." And then Jared winked at me.

"Look, thanks for your help," I said, looking first at Jared and then at Billy. "But Marcia and I need to do some planning before fifth hour. *Alone*."

Billy caught on and left, but Jared lingered. "If there's anything I can do to help, just let me know, okay?" He was pouring it on unbelievably thick. The old junior-high days came rushing back in my mind.

"Thanks, Jared. I'll let you know."

He beamed, eyes twinkling. What a goof. Jared Wilkins, it was clear, was desperate. I, however, couldn't wait to go home and reread my letters from Sean.

♥   ♥   ♥

All the studying in the world couldn't help me on Wednesday, not the way I was floundering. Andie was right. Pop quiz it was. And in spite of my frantic heavenly pleas, I flunked. Flat out.

Two days later, on Friday, Mr. Irving, my home-room teacher, handed out six-week deficiency reports as discreetly as possible. Deficient wasn't exactly the best word to describe how I felt. I avoided Andie and all my other friends as best I could throughout the rest of the day. But just as classes were finally over and I was about to escape, I bumped into Ryan Davis as I turned the corner near the administration office.

"Hey, Holly," he said, his eyes bright and his voice too loud. "How's the column?"

"No time to talk." I glanced in all directions. "You haven't seen me—remember that." I rushed for the front doors and slipped unnoticed out of school.

I was the first of the freshmen to board the city bus. Hiding in the backseat wasn't my style, but it was the only way. The only other option was walking home, but the high school was quite a ways from my house.

Mom and Uncle Jack would have a cow over this, I was certain. Fs weren't acceptable in our family. God's people put their best feet forward—they were to make a practice of excellence. Mom would be howling the loudest. And I braced myself for the barrage of inquiry.

Stealthily I crept into the house, hoping to avoid an immediate confrontation from the powers that be. But wonder of wonders, Mom wasn't even home.

"She's at a doctor's appointment," Phil, the

know-it-all brousin, informed me. "Simply routine, I suppose."

Phil . . .

Just looking at him gave me the heebie-jeebies. His new wire-rim glasses drooped almost off the tip of his oily nose. Really disgusting. But more than his appearance, his attitude bugged me. Thank goodness Mrs. Franklin was not inclined to phone my home and suggest to my parents that Phil tutor me. The way she'd left things, I figured it was up to me to pursue the tutoring business. Whew!

Honestly, I couldn't imagine sitting down with my greasy-faced brousin over algebra. Not for one single second.

Silently, I went to the hall closet and hung up my jacket, keeping my distance. Between glances at the kitchen where Phil and now Carrie, Stephie, and Mark were gathering, raiding the fridge, I felt in my jeans pocket for the dreaded deficiency report. Nothing, absolutely nothing, could be worse than having an F incubating—and in the first six weeks of high school.

I sighed, almost wishing for the old days when I would come home from school to encounter only my blood sister, Carrie. On desperate days like this, I needed peace. Time to contemplate. Time to devise plans and strategies. There were so many kids hanging out in our kitchen these days. *Our* kitchen— Mom's, Carrie's, and mine.

Nearly one year had passed since Mom had said "I do"—on Thanksgiving Day, of all things. And in that year, we'd made an attempt at blending two families—six kids, to boot. Unfortunately, one of those kids happened to be a walking, breathing, theory-developing egghead. How *had* his name shown up on Mrs. Franklin's list of tutors? He was only a sixth grader, for pete's sake!

"Hey, Holly, there's another letter from your wannabe-boyfriend," Carrie called from the kitchen.

"Why, you!" I flounced through the kitchen to the corner desk, sending fiery darts her way. "You're not supposed to touch my mail."

"I didn't even *breathe* on it." She glanced up from her bowl of ice cream. "Do I look stupid?"

"Whoa, leading question," Mark said, laughing.

"Just keep your nose out of it," I told him.

Phil ignored us, reading *The Wall Street Journal* while woofing down bites of a club sandwich. Mark, however, persisted. "Carrie's sick of being on restriction," he teased. "Every time the phone rings, she salivates."

Stephie let out a hyena shriek. "Big double woo!"

"Hush," I said, threatening both Mark and Stephie with my pointer finger. *Big double woo!* I wished Stan were home; then he could handle this, since most of the kids cluttering up the kitchen were *his* annoying little siblings.

Stephie wouldn't stop giggling, driving me crazy.

I lost it. "Stephie, puh-leeze!"

She stopped long enough to sneer. "Who died and made you boss?"

"Okay, fine. Have it your way," I said, throwing my hands up. "If this kitchen's still a mess when

Mom gets home, I'll tell her exactly who's responsible."

"Hey, don't forget what Sean wrote in his last letter," Carrie jeered. "You know, how he said—"

I clapped my hand over her sassy little mouth. "That's enough."

"What? What?" Stephie was jumping around. "What did your boyfriend say?"

"Never mind." I squinted my eyes at both Carrie and Stephie the way Mom does when she means business.

I wasn't kidding, and Carrie knew it. She squirmed away from my grasp. "I'm outta here," she said. "Homework calls."

Phil chimed in as Carrie and Stephie made their exit. "Like Mark said, Carrie's sick of being on restriction." He folded the paper and placed it in front of him. Then, without pushing up his glasses, he cast his academic gaze on me.

"So you *were* listening," I said, baffled at his ability to concentrate on multiple levels.

He nodded without blinking. "Mind-boggling, isn't it?"

I didn't want to admit it. Not now, when things were going so rotten for me.

"It's a lonely road," he blurted. "People don't understand a kid like me." I might've actually felt a tad sorry for my response, except the whiz-geek finished his remarks by saying, "At least my place in history is invulnerable."

Invulnerable? Spare me.

I clutched the letter from Sean Hamilton. Thank

goodness for a few sane males left in the world.

Instead of going upstairs to my room, I left the kitchen and my dazed brousin and went outside. The porch swing looked inviting and quiet enough for reading letters . . . and making plans. Plans such as how and when to spring my six-week report on Mom and Uncle Jack.

But first, I needed a reprieve. Sean's letter was just that. An escape from my dismal life.

8

Dear Holly,

Hey! Your letter arrived in only two days. The mail between Colorado and California is getting speedier. Sounds like things are going great for you so far your freshman year.

Yeah, I thought, wouldn't he be surprised?

I've been helping organize a new program for middle schoolers at my church. I'm on the youth board now, along with everything else. We're starting something really cool every other Friday night beginning next weekend. It's called Power House, and I'll be hanging out with sixth through eighth graders.

Does your church group zero in on younger teens? If so, I'd like to hear about it. Maybe get some ideas.

Anyway, how's your column writing coming along? Do you like reading the letters from students? Any interesting stuff?

Yeah, I wanted to send him an email message

about the mysterious letter writer with a fetish for Ws. I wanted to include it in my very first column. Maybe because it was so quirky.

I finished reading the letter, smiling at the way Sean wrapped things up.

> *When are you coming out to visit your dad again? Christmas, maybe? I miss you a lot, Holly.*
>
> *Yours, Sean*
>
> *P.S. Mr. Fremont, my calculus teacher, is almost finished with his chemo treatments. He and I had a soda after school yesterday. We talked about God again. He's so open to spiritual things. Terminal illness has a way of doing that, I suppose.*
>
> *—S.H.*

I refolded the letter and placed it back in the envelope. So much of what Sean had written stuck in my brain—his involvement with the youth group, his ongoing interest in my writing, and his strong Christian witness. But something else hit home, something I'd totally spaced out before. He was taking calculus—an advanced form of mathematics.

Would Sean consider tutoring me by email? I knew long-distance calls were out of the question. But, yeah . . . email was perfect.

In my excitement, I moved too quickly and nearly fell off the porch swing. My cat wasn't as lucky—Goofey flew onto the wooden floor, whining his dissatisfaction.

"Sorry, baby." I leaned down to pick him up.

Me-e-e-ow! He was obviously peeved. Being thrust out of a cozy spot was no fun.

I carried Goofey into the house, kissing his fat kitty head, all the while thinking of my latest plan to salvage my algebra grade. Sean as my tutor would be fabulous. Now, if I could just get my mind focused enough to write my *Dear Holly* column for the school paper. Yep, I'd decided to leave off the nickname Holly-Heart and go with something less gimmicky. Something direct.

Heading upstairs, I remembered Andie's words to me a week ago. She'd wholeheartedly suggested that I join the procrastinators of the world. Well, with this being Friday night and Marcia Greene wanting my column polished and ready to go by Monday— I'd say this was as good a procrastination stunt as any.

I chose to sit at my computer to write, even though my comfortable window seat beckoned. Goofey blinked his eyes at me from the pillowed perch, pleading for some additional cuddle time.

"Sorry, not now, baby." I reached over and nuzzled his fat neck. "Maybe later." Goofey curled his tail around his front paws and settled down for a contented snooze. End of discussion.

The first letter I picked out of the stack was Andie's. It was the off-the-wall letter she'd told me about. The one to keep me on my editorial toes . . .

Dear Holly-Heart, great imparter of human wisdom,
(I nearly choked at the salutation.)

> *Can you believe it? My locker is so messy I couldn't find my algebra homework. I mean, this is a HUGE problem. Remember how disgusting my*

locker always looked in junior high?

People say, "Less stuff means less mess," but where do I start? I mean, it's too embarrassing for the freshman class president to set up a garage sale in front of her locker.

Help me, Holly! (You're so-o-o organized.)

Signed,

Andie Martinez

P.S. Please don't edit this letter, if you know what I mean.

I couldn't help myself. I laughed out loud, waking Goofey up once again. After a quick apology to my fussy feline, I began writing my answer. A best friend's letter to the editor had to get chosen for publication. It was expected, and I knew Andie would be more than hurt if I failed her.

Picking up a pencil, I gave her my best editorial reply, keeping personal comments to a minimum.

Dear Andie,

There are a zillion ways for a person to create a sense of order in her life. Begin by simply marching up to your locker with a sense of determination. (You want to clean up and throw out, right?)

Start by labeling three large plastic bags—Give Away, Trash, and Garage Sale (thought you were kidding?). Now comes the easy part. Remove things from your locker one by one.

If you don't want or need it and it's useless, toss it. If someone else could use it and you don't want it, put it in the Give Away bag. If you think you can make some bucks on it, but you don't want it, well, there's your first garage sale item.

Remember, the hardest part is opening your locker—be sure to duck!

Happy organizing,
Holly

I reread my answer. It was okay. Might need a little rewriting, but for a first draft, not bad.

Reaching for the stack of letters, I pulled out the weird business envelope next. Now for a real challenge. This writer, whoever he/she was, wanted personal answers. Hmm, let's see . . . What should I write?

I flexed my fingers and began typing.

Dear Who Am I?:
First of all, my nickname is off-limits to strangers. Secondly, my mother gave it to me because I was born on Valentine's Day. And last but not least, you're nosy!

Sincerely, Holly
P.S. Oh—you'll receive this answer when I'm good and ready. And WHERE will it be in my column? WHO says I'm even going to publish it?!

I reread my clever letter and—having second thoughts—I decided *not* publishing it was the best answer for the Who-person.

9

I cuddled with Goofey as promised. I needed to kill some time until my parents arrived home. Hopefully Uncle Jack would get here first. Of the two, he was less inclined to freak out over my lousy math report. But that wasn't saying much. Uncle Jack wasn't a full-blown perfectionist, but he was adamant about his kids doing well in school.

My birth father was the same way if I remember correctly. It's hard to recall those long-ago days. I'm just thankful to have the kind of relationship I have with him now. It was tough going for years—the silent years—when Daddy never kept in touch with Carrie or me.

"Holly," Stan called from downstairs. The oldest Patterson sibling had arrived.

I hurried to the top of the stairs. "It's about time you're home."

He waved a paper in his hand on the landing below. "Lose something?"

Yikes! I ran downstairs, reaching for the paper, hoping it wasn't what I thought. "Give it to me," I demanded.

He held it higher. "Man, are you in for it big," he taunted, playing keep-away. "And I mean big." After repeated pleading on my part, Stan relinquished the deficiency report.

"Where'd you find this?" I caught my breath.

He pointed to the living room. "Right there on the floor in plain view."

I groaned. It must've fallen out of my pocket when I carried Goofey inside.

"Guess who's gonna be grounded next," Stan sang as he shuffled through the dining room to the kitchen.

I followed him. "You don't know that."

"Dream on, Meredith."

"Don't call me that!"

"It's your name, isn't it?" He poured a tall glass of milk, mocking me.

"Hey, save some milk for Goofey," I said, trying to divert the conversation.

"Goofey *Meredith?* You bet!"

I wanted to scream. This stepsibling was the worst.

"So . . . when do you plan to break the news to the chain of command?" Stan scoffed.

"Don't be disrespectful to our parents."

He slapped some turkey slices on a piece of bread, then squirted mustard all over before putting the sandwich together. He raised one eyebrow. "You *are* going to tell them, aren't you?"

"None of your business." I stomped out of the room.

Upstairs, I headed for the hall phone. Andie was someone I could call and dump on. Maybe even get a little sympathy, too. At least she'd offer a little understanding.

"Martinez residence," she answered.

"Hey, why so formal?"

"Oh, you know. It's proper."

I got the strong feeling her mom was in close proximity. "Can you talk?"

"Uh . . . sure."

"Depending on what it is, right?"

"You got it." I could just imagine Andie grinning into the phone.

"So . . . what's going on?" I asked.

"Oh, not much. You?"

"To tell the truth, I'm seeing purple about now," I complained. "Your former boyfriend and my present brousin are driving me nuts."

"Uh-oh, what'd Stanley Patterson do now?"

"He found my *deficiency* report," I said, reluctantly at first. "Bottom line: If he tells Mom and Uncle Jack about it before I do, I'll deprive him of his old age."

"Wait a minute," she interrupted. "Did you say deficiency report?"

"I wondered if you were paying attention."

"Oh, good, so it's really not that."

"Worse," I confessed. "I'm flunking algebra, and Mrs. Franklin is suggesting a tutor." I didn't tell her who, of course.

"Flunking? That's rough."

"Do you know any tutors my age?"

"Well, yeah . . . I think so."

"Please don't suggest Billy. Not because he isn't smart enough; it's just not fair, you know, the way he—"

"But wait, Holly. Maybe Billy wouldn't be such a bad idea."

I could almost hear the romantic ideas buzzing in her brain. "You're supposed to be on *my* side," I said.

"It's just that Billy would be so fabulous for you—if I can use your word."

"Billy?"

"Think about it. Billy's right here—in Dressel Hills."

Oh, not this again, I thought. "Look, I don't need another lecture about long-distance relationships, okay? That's up to me to decide."

"Why can't you see the light, Holly? Besides, Billy's really hurt."

"Why? I don't get it . . . I mean, what's changed?" I said. "I think he's great . . . as a friend. Just like always."

"To tell you the truth, I promised to help him," she finally admitted.

"To set him up with me? C'mon!"

There was unbearable silence on the line. Andie snapped to it at last. "Well, I think I hear my mom calling. It's almost supper and I have to help. See ya."

"Okay." I hung up the phone feeling worse than ever.

10

By the time both Mom and Uncle Jack were home, it was suppertime. No one, at least none of us kids, had taken the initiative to prepare anything.

"I'll cook," Uncle Jack volunteered. He rubbed his hands together as though doing so might start a roaring campfire.

I laughed. "This isn't the Boy Scouts." I reached for the largest pot in the house. "I'll cook tonight. How's spaghetti?"

"That's my Holly-Heart," Mom said, smiling weakly. She leaned against the kitchen counter. For the first time, I noticed how gaunt her face looked.

"Mom, are you okay?" I asked.

"Don't be silly." She seemed apologetic. Uncle Jack went over and put his arm around her, leading her into the living room. Now I was worried. Wasn't it a week ago we had pizza because Mom was too tired to make supper?

This just wasn't Mom. Not the hardworking

mother who'd been a paralegal all those years to sup-
port Carrie and me after Daddy left.

I sprinkled salt into the water and turned the
burner on high. Then I filled Goofey's dish with his
favorite liver and tuna cat food and refilled his milk
dish. A glance toward the living room filled me in
on Mom's status. She was resting her head on Uncle
Jack's shoulder. A good sign for not-so-newlyweds, I
guess. Only thing, Uncle Jack was reading the paper,
not stroking her hair and saying sweet nothings. So
what was I to think? Was Mom sick or just tired?

Not only was I worried about Mom, I was appre-
hensive about when to share the horrors of my six-
week report. I certainly didn't want to make her feel
worse. But if I didn't tell, would Stan jump the gun?
What if I didn't tell at all? Who would sign on the
parental line?

Maybe after supper and devotions I could get
Uncle Jack off by himself. Besides, I needed to find
out what he thought about linking up with an elec-
tronic tutor. Namely Sean Hamilton.

♥   ♥   ♥

My spaghetti dinner turned out fine; so did devotions. Sorta. We sat around the living room in a hap-
hazard circle. Uncle Jack read several Bible passages.
One verse really touched me. Second Corinthians
12:9—"My grace is sufficient for you, for my power
is made perfect in weakness."

Wow! Did that mean God was going to give me grace to bear the hardships of algebra? Was He also going to make a way to escape? No, that was another verse.

My grace is sufficient. I had to cling to that promise. I was a child of God. I was entitled to this verse—to make it mine.

Later, Uncle Jack asked if any of us had something to pray about. Carrie's hand shot up, and I wondered what she was going to say. "We need to pray for Sean in California," she said, avoiding my glare.

"Oh?" Uncle Jack said. "Why is that?" I held my breath. What would she say?

"Well, it's like this," she began. "He's been writing to Holly, you know, and—"

"Carrie," Mom interjected, "is this really something to be discussed in front of the family?"

Hooray for Mom!

Carrie frowned.

"Is this a prayer request or not?" Uncle Jack continued where Mom left off.

"Well, yeah, *I* think it is." Carrie's face wore an impish, triumphant look.

I cast a stern eye on my younger sister. She dropped it immediately. "Uh . . . never mind," she stammered.

Uncle Jack ran his fingers through his wavy brown hair, looking a bit confused. "Anyone else?"

Phil's hand went up. "Pray that I'll fit in with the rest of the seventh graders at my school. This Monday I'm getting bumped out of sixth grade."

Shoot, this was no prayer request. The little know-it-all was showing off. What nerve—announcing his skip to seventh grade like this.

"Well, congratulations, son," Uncle Jack said, getting caught up in the whole thing. If Mom hadn't prompted him back on course, our family prayers might've gotten preempted by Phil's tales of accomplishment.

After we took turns praying around the circle (I prayed for Mom in general terms since I didn't know if she'd fallen prey to the flu or what), I followed Uncle Jack around the house. Discreetly as possible, of course. I hoped, and silently prayed, that I'd have a chance to discuss my algebra plight with him. The way things were going, though, it looked like I'd be stuck worrying the whole weekend. Why? Because Phil had become the focus of Uncle Jack's attention. Not that it was so bad, but it left me out in the cold. Way out.

One look at Mom, sprawled out comfortably on the couch, and I knew she wasn't up to being told. Fs stood for failure. I certainly felt like one tonight. Especially pitted against the atmosphere of genius pervading the house.

My grace is sufficient for you . . .

"Please, send down your grace, Lord," I prayed as I headed for my room. Here I was, facing another Friday night of solitude. Not lonely, I didn't mean that. I had Sean's letters and the memories we'd made together last summer to keep me company.

My *Dear Holly* column was basically written, and I had hardly any other homework to do. Except algebra. That would have to wait.

I turned on my CD player and found my yellow spiral notebook. Its pages held the first novel I'd ever attempted to write. It would be a novella—a mini novel. I nestled down with my cat on my window seat, pushing out my worries as I began to round off a scene in the second chapter. That done, I reread what I'd written, then erased several words and chose stronger verbs and fewer adjectives. This time, when I read it, I was satisfied.

Over an hour had gone by when I reached for a Marty Leigh mystery and began to read. I figured if I was going to be a great writer, I had to read the best authors. Ms. Leigh certainly fit that description.

Unfortunately, in the book I chose—in the very first chapter—the main character had an aversion to math. Nope, this would never do. Too close to home, so I closed the book.

Frustrated, I went to my bottom dresser drawer and pulled out my journal. *Friday night, October 18: I hope to talk to Uncle Jack first thing tomorrow . . . give him the news that I'm flunking algebra. It won't be easy, but nothing like this ever is. Then, before he has a chance to freak out, I'll tell him my plan to link up with Sean as my tutor. Or . . . maybe I could tell him about my tutor plan BEFORE I say anything about the deficiency report. Yeah, that's better. Hey, perfect! God's grace is beginning to work for me. Now, if I can just make it through tomorrow.*

11

Saturday I got up, showered, and dressed long before any other kids in the house were up. I fixed my hair, too. I wanted to look as though I was in complete control of my senses when I sprang the email tutoring idea on Uncle Jack.

Mom was stirring up a bowl of waffle batter when I sailed into the kitchen. "Morning, angel." Her voice sounded sweet, strong.

"Feeling better?" I asked, stealing a glance at Uncle Jack, who was spooning sugar into his coffee.

"Much," Mom answered, though preoccupied.

Uncle Jack looked up. "A good night's sleep changes everyone's outlook. Right, hon?"

She turned, smiling across the room.

Perfect, I thought. *Mom's rested up . . . Uncle Jack's had his first cup of coffee . . .*

I dragged a bar stool across the floor and sat at the corner of the island, kitty-corner from Uncle Jack. "Got a minute?"

Uncle Jack winked at me. "For you, sweet toast, I've got all day. What's up?"

"I have a fabulous idea . . . to pull up my algebra grade."

"I'm all for pulling up grades." He nodded, listening.

"Well, since mine's a little low, and since my friend Sean Hamilton is taking calculus, well . . . I just thought maybe I could correspond with him about my homework and stuff."

"How low a grade are we talking?" he asked.

Rats! I had no choice but to turn over the deficiency report. This conversation was going backward. I sighed.

"C'mon, out with the whole truth," Uncle Jack said, his jovial smile fading fast. Mom came and peered over his shoulder.

Doomsday!

True to form, Mom was the first to react after she saw the report. "My goodness, Holly, you've never had an F!"

"I know. And I feel rotten about it. That's why I want to get help."

"You could have asked your mother or me for help," Uncle Jack was saying.

"Why did you wait till you were failing to tell us about this?" Mom asked.

Questions, questions. I felt like an idiotic lump. In fact, I had a strong desire to limp out of the room. Away from all this pressure. Show them how lousy they were making me feel.

"Holly?" Mom persisted.

"I've been trying to raise my grade, really. But the problem is, I don't understand algebra. It's like a *foreign* foreign language." I had to say that, because I was making A's in my French class. "Besides, I didn't want to bother you with my schoolwork. I didn't think it was fair." I didn't want to look like a dodo bird next to my super-intelligent brousin, either.

Phil and Mark trooped into the kitchen, still wearing their pajamas. Hair askew, they headed for Mom's mixing bowl. "I'm starved," Mark said. He threatened to poke his finger in the batter.

"When's breakfast?" Phil asked.

Mom rushed over to the counter and shooed the boys away, continuing her Saturday morning ritual. Without looking over her shoulder, she spoke to the wall. "Well, something's got to be done about this, Holly."

Phil's ears perked up. "Is this about grades?"

Uncle Jack held up his hand. "No concern of yours. You boys go and wash up."

"But Dad," Phil continued, "If it's math we're talking about, I can help Holly. I know I can."

Gulp!

Uncle Jack kept talking to me, as though he hadn't heard Phil's comment. "I really think getting Sean involved is a mistake. He's a junior this year, right?"

I nodded.

"And he's taking calculus?"

"He's really smart," I pleaded my case. "He's headed for pre-med . . . wants to be a doctor."

"Which means he's probably loaded up with homework of his own," Uncle Jack argued.

Phil stood by, as though waiting for a lull in the conversation. "I'm on the school district's tutor list," he volunteered. "My teacher signed me up to help math students. I'll get extra credit for it."

I held my breath. Hoping . . . no, *praying* that Uncle Jack wouldn't consider such a ridiculous idea.

"You're a tutor?" A proud smile burst upon Uncle Jack's face, and he grabbed Phil's arm and hugged him. "Well, what do you know. When did all this happen?"

Phil grinned. "About two weeks ago. Except I haven't been assigned to anyone yet."

Yeah, and over my dead body do you get extra credit from me, I thought, refusing to look at the geeky little Einstein.

"Well, maybe it's time for your first assignment," I heard Uncle Jack say. "Your mom or I could help Holly, but it would be much better—great experience—coming from you."

I bit my lip. "Please, no, Uncle Jack." I wanted to say more. Something like, what have I done to deserve this? Phil smirked mischievously behind his father's back.

I felt the urge to choke him. Phil was making a fool of me!

"I can find someone else—honest, I can," I pleaded.

"Oh, now, let's not get melodramatic about this, Holly," Uncle Jack teased.

Didn't he realize how upset I was?

"How would *you* like to be tutored by . . . by . . ."
I couldn't finish. Phil was enjoying this whole nightmarish scene. I couldn't stomach it. Or him.

Unfortunately Uncle Jack wasn't registering my
complaint. Not even close. He got up and went over
to Mom and nibbled on her ear. "What do you
think, hon? Should we let my son tutor your daughter?" It was like they had something secretive going
on between them.

Mom plugged in the waffle iron. "Why not? Give
it a try—say, two weeks. See how they work
together."

My heart sank to my tennies. Work together—
with Philip Patterson, smart-alecky brousin and big-
time troublemaker? There was major potential here,
all right.

Potential for a nuclear explosion!

Bad news travels fast. In small mountain towns, in major cities. Doesn't matter. If there's something bad to be said about someone, you can bet someone's willing to talk about it. Starting with my meeting with Marcia Greene first thing Monday.

Instead of discussing the upcoming paper, Marcia brought up the algebra thing—and my new student instructor. "Word has it you're being tutored by a younger sibling." She sounded like something straight out of CNN.

"And?" I said.

Marcia frowned. "There's more?"

"Well, I sure hope not," I muttered. "I'll never live this one down—a freshman flunky with her eleven-year-old brousin for a tutor."

"Brousin?" Marcia looked very confused.

I shook my head. "Never mind; it's a long story." I showed her the nutty letter from "Who Am I?" She read it quickly. "This guy's a loony tune."

"If you think his letter's strange, you should read my reply."

She nearly doubled over as she read my answer. "This is really great stuff, Holly." She read it once more. "I say we publish it."

"Fat chance getting Mrs. Ross to agree."

"You might be surprised. What do you say?" She waited for my answer while her fingers drummed lightly on the desk.

"Uh . . . I don't know," I hedged.

"C'mon, it shows off your uncommonly creative talents." She shuffled through my pages of responses to the last several weeks of student letters. "This *Dear Holly* column is going to be a big hit. I can't wait till the November issue screams off the press."

I was thinking about the weird writer again. "Are you sure you want to run that 'Who Am I?' letter with my response?"

"No doubt in my mind. You're good, Holly. Let's get the column off to a wild and fantastic start."

"Fabulous," I said, not sure I meant it.

♥　♥　♥

In a few hours, most of Dressel Hills had heard some version of my academic plight. But the most messed-up paraphrase came from my sister Carrie.

"You've got to be kidding," I told her at home. "You repeated something that stupid?"

Carrie didn't mind rehashing totally twisted

accounts of my personal life. She seemed to live and breathe for such things—now that she was ten. "Well, the way I heard it, you were pleading with Phil to help you with your algebra," she said. "And since he needed the extra credit, he caved in and agreed."

"That's ridiculous, and you know it."

"Well, I didn't actually witness what happened last Saturday. It's really your word against everyone else's." Carrie tossed her waist-length blond hair in defiance.

"Wrong again," I muttered, heading for the dining room.

My eleven-year-old tutor was perched in the chair where Uncle Jack always sat during meals, awaiting our first session. Believe me, if Mom and several other members of the family hadn't been in close range, I'd have smashed my algebra book over his pointed little egghead!

Phil waited till I sat down to speak. "To begin with," he said all hoity-toity, "I think you probably need to review some basic arithmetic."

Arithmetic? Who was he kidding?

"Look, for your information, I can add, subtract, multiply, and divide just fine." I restrained myself, eyeing Mom every so often as she sat in the living room sipping peppermint tea.

"A quick review can't hurt," Phil persisted.

"Can't help, either," I argued. "Not when it's *algebra* I don't understand."

"Okay, have it your way." He actually stopped diagnosing my math problems.

I opened to last week's homework pages. "Here's what I have to do over. Mrs. Franklin said so." By throwing around my teacher's name, I hoped Phil would stop acting like such an obnoxious boss. Because, in the long run, *she* was the person really in charge of all this tutoring business. I curled my toes, remembering the weird scene in Mrs. Franklin's class today after school. Phil had come to meet her (and to be coached about my homework problems) while I sat there in total humiliation.

Hearing Phil articulate on the same intellectual level with Mrs. Franklin, made me feel . . . well, inadequate. That feeling, however, disappeared the second we set foot in the house. Here at home, I was not going to be intimidated by my little brousin's IQ. He had a lot to learn when it came to dealing with a big sister, and like it or not, I was going to have the last word.

The two of us hung on as long as possible, but when it came to working on actual problems, I couldn't take his arrogance. Sure, he was bright, and yes, he understood all this mathematical hodge-podge—but that sneer! And those cocky, superior grins. His attitude angered me—made me resent what he was trying to do. So our first tutoring session fizzled after about fifteen minutes.

"I have an idea," Phil said as I stood up to go to my room. "Why don't you just ask for help when you get stuck? I'll be right here doing a memory experiment."

I pounced on his verbal niceties. "And I'll be making reservations for intergalactic travel," I huffed, then dashed up the stairs.

"Holly!" Mom called. "Come down here."

I stopped at the top of the stairs. "Mom, he's driving me crazy."

"Let's talk," she said, standing firm.

I shuffled back down and sat on the bottom step, pouting. "It's not working. He's impossible."

Phil blinked his eyes like a lizard. One of his most disgusting attempting-to-appear-innocent routines. "We can't give up on the first day," he said.

"Oh, yeah? Watch me."

Mom put her hand on my shoulder. "The two of you need time to adjust. I think after several more sessions, things could fall into place. Holly-Heart, won't you give it another try?" She was trying so hard to smooth out the rough edges. Mom was a true peacemaker.

Lizard Phil blinked again, his eyelids coming down like shutters. Made me livid.

I stood up. "Not now. I've had it for today."

Once again I left the room, taking the stairs two at a time. Goofey ran up after me and clawed at my bedroom door. I endured his stubborn meowing for several seconds, then let him in.

"Life's the pits." I tossed my algebra book on my lavender-and-lace canopy bed and pulled out my journal. If I didn't unload my feelings soon, I knew I would explode.

Monday, October 21: I don't know what to do! Having my stepbrother as a math tutor is absolutely horrible. It's worse than I thought! I wish I could get past his puffed-up demeanor.

It's true, I need help—Mrs. Franklin won't let me forget that fact. Besides that, I almost lost it today when Phil started conversing with her like he was applying for a teacher's aide position or something. It's tough keeping my cool when what I really want to do is wring his little neck!

Praying is what I need to do right now. But it's not like I haven't been talking to God. I have. Being patient isn't always easy. And the grace—where's the grace?

Sometimes I think I'm a lousy Christian. Especially when I lose my temper and blow up at my own family members.

Surely Jesus never went off on one of His own brothers. I'm trying to be loving . . . and failing. Lord, help me. Please.

13

Tuesday morning before school, a note was stuck on my locker. I surveyed the area, checking to see if anyone was observing—someone who might've planted the note. In the sea of student humanity, no one stood out as looking suspicious.

Marcia Greene and her brother, Zye, and his tagalong, Ryan, were heading down the hall. I figured they didn't count, and everyone else was pretty much minding his own business.

I opened my locker and leaned inside a bit, shielding the note from prying eyes. Quickly, I opened it and began to read.

Dear Holly,

So you're going to publish my letter—and your response to it—in the next issue of The Summit. *WHERE do you think my words will appear in your column? And WHAT did I do to deserve such an honor? (Heh, heh.)*

Certainly, I'll be eager to see if you answered all

*my questions—the 5 Ws are so important to good
journalism. Oh, yes, and 1 H (HOW), don't forget.*

HOW did you get to be so pretty?

Signed: WHO am I?

P.S. WHY did you cut your beautiful hair?

I crumpled up the note and threw it into my
locker. Whoever this was . . . he was out there.

Gathering up my books for the morning classes,
I closed my locker and headed for my first-hour class.
Government.

Jared Wilkins was waiting for me just inside the
door. "I'm real sorry to hear what's going on at
home," he began. "A girl like you shouldn't have to
put up with a little brother for a—"

"Save it, Wilkins." I pushed past him and found
a seat close to the front of the classroom.

"Holly, what's wrong?" I heard him say. "I can
help you. I'm pulling an A right now in algebra." He
sat behind me, ranting about his incredible tutoring
abilities.

"Too bad everyone in Dressel Hills has to mind
my business," I mumbled into my backpack, searching for the textbook.

Jared touched my shoulder, and reluctantly I
turned around. He flashed his dazzling smile. "I'm
offering my services, Holly. No strings attached."

A *first*, I thought, pulling a smirk.

"Seriously," he continued, "if you want help with
algebra, I'm here for you."

"Thanks, but no thanks."

"Well, I don't believe for one minute that you're

okay with having a fledgling brother tutor you."

"I'll survive." The class was filling up, and I didn't care to pursue the conversation further. I turned back around, facing the front.

Jared tried to push the issue, but I refused to budge in his direction. I opened the textbook, grateful to be pulling top grades in *this* class.

♥   ♥   ♥

When the bell rang at the end of first hour, I noticed Billy and Andie together in the back of the room. "Yo, Holly!" Andie called. "Come here a sec."

Jared, flirty as ever, was attempting to get my attention again. I ignored him and hurried to see what Andie wanted. "Hey," I said, looking first at Andie, then at Billy.

"Hey, Holly," Billy's voice was hardly more than a whisper. Laryngitis, maybe?

"I'll leave now," Andie said, grinning at me. "Billy wants to talk to you." And with that, she left.

The little sneak.

I stood there feeling awkward. Billy coughed a little. "Got a cold?" I asked, trying to break the ice.

"Not really." He looked uncomfortable, right down to his sneakers.

"Look, did Andie put you up to this?" I asked.

He shrugged. "I wouldn't say that."

"Then, what *would* you say? I mean, about Andie. Is she trying to get you to do something for her—about me, I mean?" I was remembering that she bristled every time I mentioned Sean. The long-distance letter-writing thing really bugged her.

"Don't blame Andie." Billy looked me square in the face. "I really wanted to talk to you, uh, about some . . . some other stuff."

I was getting antsy. We only had five minutes for passing periods between classes. If we were late, there was a pink slip. Three pink slips equaled after-school detention. With a temporary F in algebra, I couldn't afford even the tiniest flaw on my high-school record.

I glanced at the wall clock. "Okay, we can talk sometime. When?"

"After school?"

"Where?"

"Soda Straw okay?" he asked.

I almost said, Why? but decided I was sounding like the nut who'd written the weird letters.

Then it hit me, and I probably stared at him. Could Billy Hill be the letter writer? I mean, he was obviously infatuated or whatever. But would Billy really do something that dumb? I couldn't imagine it, but I was sure I could devise a plan to test my suspicions.

I eyed the clock. "We better get going. See you after school." I rushed off to choir.

The risers were filling up when I arrived. Andie was perched on the piano bench, waiting for Mrs. Duncan, the director. Andie's face lit up when she saw me.

I slid onto the piano bench and gave her a

nudge. "Hey, girl," I whispered, "what are you trying to do? About Billy, I mean."

"Nothing."

"Think again," I said. "You're doing something weird—and using Billy in the process. I just know it."

Andie offered a frown. "I can't believe you think that."

"Truth hurts."

Mrs. Duncan arrived, carrying her burlap shoulder bag crammed with music. I hurried to my place on the risers, next to the Miller twins—Paula and Kayla, sophomores.

"You're tardy," Paula said smugly, and I smirked at her choice of words. Paula and Kayla both had a strange way with the English language.

"Not actually late," I countered. "Just close."

Paula rolled her eyes. She was obviously ticked at me. And I was sure it had nothing to do with tardiness. More than likely, Billy Hill.

"Look, Paula, if you think I'm moving in on your guy, you're wrong."

She was silent.

"But . . ." I hesitated, thinking ahead. "I think you should know that he and I plan to meet somewhere to talk after school. It's Billy's idea," I explained, in no uncertain terms. Paula, after all, was a good friend; it had taken a long time for us to get to a decent level of rapport. I wasn't going to let Billy's present insanity interfere. Besides, I wanted Paula to know I wasn't sneaking around behind her back.

"It's really none of my concern," Paula replied. "What Billy does with his leisure time is entirely optional."

Sounded like Paula and Billy might actually be history. No wonder Andie was pushing Billy to link up with me. It was perfect from her standpoint. Get Holly to fall for Billy and . . . *au revoir* to Sean.

But why was Andie so set on the demise of Sean and me? I made a mental note to ask her.

Mrs. Duncan located her director's copies of several songs, then she took the podium. "Sorry about the delay," she said, adjusting her glasses. "Now . . . will the section leaders please pass these songs around?" She held up three of my favorites. One was from the musical *Cats*, titled, "Jellicle Songs for Jellicle Cats."

We rehearsed parts on the first piece, then put the harmonies together. Paula, however, was barely singing. At least, not in her usual robust manner. I could tell she wasn't just a little ticked over this thing with Billy. Of course, she would never admit it. Not in a zillion years.

I tried to honey-coat things over after choir by offering to sit with her at lunch. She had other plans. "Kayla and I are eating together today, but thanks." She glanced at her twin, who was gathering up the sheet music. The two of them were dressed exactly alike with matching denim jean skirts and red polo shirts. It struck me as highly unusual since they'd been working so hard to establish their separate identities. Then Paula turned to me unexpectedly. "Did you get the letter I wrote, you know, for the editorial column?"

"I haven't checked my mail yet today, but I will." Then another idea came to me. "Did you sign your name to your letter?"

"Well, why not?" she said in a huff. "Of course I did. I don't have anything to hide."

I nodded. "I didn't mean to imply that, Paula. It's just that I keep getting these strange letters from someone who never signs off with a real name."

"Really?" Her eyes grew wide. "Who would do that?"

"That's what I'm trying to find out," I explained, suddenly thinking of the perfect plan. "By the way, do you think you would recognize Billy's handwriting?"

"Billy's?" She stiffened. "You think Billy's writing weird letters to the school paper?" She looked completely aghast.

"I didn't say that, did I?" It was getting close to the third-hour bell.

"No, but—"

"Would you be willing to at least take a look at one of the letters?" I asked.

"Well, I guess"—then a smile spread across her face—"if you'd be willing to do something for me."

"Anything," I said as we headed for the hallway.

"Promise you won't meet Billy after school?"

"What?" I studied her. What a strange request.

"Please?" she said, accompanied by a pained expression.

I sighed. Paula wasn't being devious. The girl was

hurt—grasping at straws to keep her guy.

"Just plain stand him up," she said. "Deal?"

This was unbelievable. "Uh, okay, you win," I said, realizing how much I needed her help. "Meet me at my locker before lunch. I'll show you the letter then."

Paula's face broke into a sunshine smile. Things seemed much better for her. But what about me? What would I tell Billy? I couldn't just not show up.

Could I?

14

Paula appeared at my locker immediately after fourth hour. I smoothed out the scrunched-up letter and she read it. "The handwriting isn't familiar to me, but that doesn't mean it's not Billy."

I was puzzled. "Why can't you be sure?"

She pushed her brunette hair behind her ears. "Billy can write with *both* hands. He's ambidextrous." She smiled as though it were some inside information, between just the two of them.

"Hmm, I never knew." I surveyed the letter. "Could it be that Billy is also two-faced?" I had to say that—had to test her loyalty.

Paula's eyebrows lurched up. "Two-faced? Not on your life."

I closed my locker door and Paula turned to go. "Wait, there's one more thing. You can't mention any of this to Billy, okay?"

She nodded. "Sure."

"And something else. I'll tell Billy that I won't

be meeting him today . . . and the reason why."

Her face turned ashen. "No, please don't. It would be a big mistake to tell him you and I talked."

"Why? Because then he'd know exactly how you *still* feel about him? Want to know what I think? I think you're crazy about him."

She shook her head. "It's not important anymore, honest." Seemed to me she was pleading.

"So . . . what really happened? To make you break up, I mean?" I probably shouldn't have stuck my nose in, but I was dying to know.

"Let's leave well enough alone," she said.

I could tell by the sad look in her eyes that the parting of ways hadn't been her idea. Which had me even more worried. Did it have something to do with Billy's silly crush on me?

Paula and I headed in opposite directions. Inside the cafeteria I felt torn up—really sorry. Especially for Paula. And now also for Billy. He'd had a difficult time getting up the nerve to ask me to meet him at the Soda Straw. And now I wouldn't be going at all. I'd made a deal with Paula, and I wouldn't think of breaking it.

Andie waved me over to her table, smack dab in the middle of zillions of people. When I sat down and started eating, she jumped all over me. "Are you out of your mind, girl?"

This line was beginning to wear thin. "What now?" I wailed.

"I saw you talking to Paula." She tilted her head toward the hallway. "Don't you know you'll mess things up between you and Billy if he sees the two of you hanging out?"

"I really don't care what Billy thinks."

She sighed and shook her head at her tray. "Don't you see? Billy's gun shy."

"What's that supposed to mean?"

"You know, it's taken him all this time to have the courage to—"

"Wait a minute," I interrupted. "*All* this time? What are we talking here, a week—ten days?"

She threw her hands up, looking completely disgusted. "I'd think you'd catch on after a while; I mean, c'mon!"

She was actually frantic. So . . . why was Andie acting so strange?

"Look, I think we need to talk about something," I said. "It's about Sean."

"Hamilton?"

I nodded. "Why are you so worried about him?"

Andie's dark eyes clouded. "You're making fun of me."

I touched her shoulder. "Don't be so sensitive."

She was quiet for a moment. Then the words "I'm afraid" slipped out of her mouth.

This was bizarre. "Afraid of what?"

"Of losing you—us," she muttered. "And don't laugh."

Again I was baffled. "You think I'm going to lose my head over Sean Hamilton? Is that it?"

She picked at her food. "Could be. After all, I did meet this amazing boyfriend of yours last summer, remember? He's a real gem, as my mom would say."

"But aren't you jumping to conclusions? I'm not even allowed to date for another four months, for pete's sake."

"But," she protested, "you can't tell me he's not thinking and probably praying, if I know Sean, about God's will for his life. Same as you, right?"

"Of course." I reached for my chicken sandwich. "But you don't have to worry *now* about that."

"You'll be going off to college in a few years."

"That's my goal." I knew she'd ruled out going, but I kept hoping maybe she'd change her mind.

"So, no matter what, we'll end up apart." She leaned her elbow on the tray, staring at me. "We really only have a short time left, you know." She sounded awfully gloomy. Almost as depressed as I'd been last month.

"Andie, you're sounding morbid. Will you quit?"

"Well, at least now you know the truth. I've been the one encouraging Billy, have been all along, hoping for a way to keep you here in Dressel Hills," she confessed. "Because if the two of you actually linked up—got married eventually, after college—Billy would probably bring his bride back home to Dressel Hills."

"There's no guarantee. You can't know what Billy or I would do after graduation—*separately!*" I said. "People move around; things change. Just because I might marry a hometown boy doesn't mean I'd live forever in this town—or even Colorado. You should know that. Besides, what if you end up marrying a guy from somewhere else?"

"I can't see that happening." She sighed. "Oh,

it's all so scary—the unknown—when you think about it."

I laughed, trying to lighten the mood. "Then quit thinking. It gets you in trouble."

She laughed, too, only not her cheerful, robust laughter.

My best friend was not only depressed over our future options, she was also becoming paranoid. I couldn't stand it—her obsession and fear of the unknown. "You really ought to get a grip on this whole future thing, Andie," I said. "Why don't you let God handle it, and mine, too, while you're at it."

"I know, I know. Just please, whatever you do, don't stand Billy up."

I shook my head. "Look, it's just this once—I have no choice."

We talked some more. And wisely, I steered the conversation away from future hopes and dreams . . . and her fears, all the way to the big math mess I was in. "So how would *you* like to be stuck having your little brother for a tutor?"

That got a sincere smile. "How's it working?"

"It's not. In fact, it's so bad I suggested we meet in a public place to avoid killing each other."

Andie twisted a curl. I should've known right then she was cooking something up in her mind. "Are you saying you'll be hanging out at the library after school today?"

I nodded. "And if you see Billy, would you mind giving him a message?"

"Like what?"

"Tell him I'm really sorry, but I can't meet him after all."

She gasped. "You're honestly breaking your first date with the poor boy?"

"It isn't a date, and Billy's not poor."

Andie frowned. "Why *are* you standing him up?"

"It's a long story."

"Oh, I know. Paula must've gotten to you."

Suddenly, I missed Tina Frazer, my blind friend. *She* wouldn't be giving me the third degree! She was as cool as you get . . . except she'd gone back to the School for the Deaf and Blind for the semester.

Andie stared at me. "Well, did she?"

"Paula?" I was tired of being interrogated. "Let's just call it a day, okay?"

Andie made a face. "Whatever."

"Ditto for me." I was maxed out with Andie.

We had an open-book test in French class and Mr. Irving was nice enough to come around and help some of us. Next class was English, and Mrs. Ross was her very cool self, encouraging several students to submit articles for *The Summit*. I secretly wondered if I'd ever be fortunate enough to have my novella published. The way I saw it, if I could just conquer my algebra problems once and for all—figure out the unknown quantities—I'd have plenty of time to work on my book.

Hey, wait a minute! I sat straight up in my desk. *The unknown.* That's what Andie was talking about at lunch. She was afraid of it. Afraid and obsessed.

Was that my problem, too—except about algebra? Was I afraid of solving unknown factors? Maybe I was causing my own mental block. Hey, this was heavy, something a shrink might come up with. But I was still in that weird stage of life when adults expected hairbrained behavior. Actually, I was close to turning fifteen.

Ah, to be fifteen, I thought. *Or sixteen, even.* The magical mid-teens when your freaking out should be limited to finding the perfect clothes to wear on your first date. None of this rebellious stuff with parents, or fighting with smart-alecky stepsiblings or even best friends. Nope, I would be breezing easy. Very soon.

Mom always said once I got past fourteen, my up-and-down emotional roller coaster would probably start to level off. I hoped she was right.

There was something else I couldn't wait for: the "Dear Holly" column, soon to be launched. It would be so fabulous to see my words in print again.

Mrs. Ross was talking to the class. "Holly, will you please distribute school papers to homerooms next week?"

I snapped out of my daze. "I'd love to."

Her round face broke into a huge grin. "I had a feeling you might." She took her place at the chalkboard, preparing to write the assignment. I thought back to seventh grade when one of the boys had made fun of the fat under her arm. It jiggled when she wrote. But not anymore. Mrs. Ross had slimmed down considerably since she'd married our former science teacher.

"Dear class," she began, as though dictating a verbal letter. As she lectured, I thought about another letter. The one I'd crumpled up and Paula had inspected. Could it be—was it possible—that Billy was the guy behind the strange letters?

Sitting there, spacing out, I wished I could take back the promise I'd made Paula. Why had she tricked me? If only I hadn't fallen for her deal. If only . . .

"Each of you will write a scene—an imaginative scenario—based on an 'If only,' " Mrs. Ross said, and it registered in my brain as I began paying attention. I was amazed at this coincidence.

Smiling, I reached for my assignment notebook and pen. *If only?* What a perfect assignment for a girl who basically lived her life around the words. Now there was another thing I couldn't wait for—the chance to sit down and begin working on Mrs. Ross's ingenious assignment.

♥   ♥   ♥

After school I found my stepbrother Phil at the library plugged into a book. I'd chosen the public library instead of the high-school library for obvious reasons.

"Let's hurry and get this over with," I whispered, pulling out a chair and arranging my books. Glancing at him, I realized it hadn't even registered with him that I was there. "Yoo-hoo, nerd-brain, your victim has arrived."

Phil lowered his book, his eyes staring blankly. "Victim? Where?" He looked around.

"Duh? Are you dense, or what?"

He shook himself back. "Now, where were we?"

"We weren't anywhere, at least not yet." I had the feeling I'd interrupted a fabulous read. I reached for his book. "What's the title?"

He showed me. *Search for the Unknown Species.*

"Sci-fi?"

He nodded. "A little out there, so to speak, but then again, maybe not as far as we think." A weird, half-baked expression flitted across his spectacled face. "You'd have to read it."

I put up my hands. "Uh, no thanks, not my genre."

"What *is* your fictional taste?"

"Oh, things like mysteries, suspense . . . and of course, a little romance mixed in." After I divulged my preferences, I realized that I'd actually lowered my guard.

"Hey, this is good." He grinned goofily. "We're making a connection."

I didn't let his remark shake me up. Honestly, I felt very weird talking to Phil at all. In public anyway. Sure, he was my blood cousin and stepbrother, but hanging out with ultimate geeks was not the best way to enhance one's high-school reputation.

High-school students comprised a rare breed. I, having been thrust into high school prematurely, was beginning to see my own metamorphosis. At times, though, I didn't like what I saw.

"Uh . . . hello, Holly?" Phil leaned forward on the table, waving his hands in my face. He was wearing a brown turtleneck, and for an instant, I thought he looked more like a *turtle* than a tutor.

"Sorry. Guess I spaced out."

"You know," he said, "since we're opening up like this, I might as well tell you something." He looked at me as though waiting for an invitation to continue.

"We're here to work on algebra."

"First, let me point out one of your bad habits." He pushed his glasses up. No, he *slid* them up, with a lot of help from the nose grease that continuously oozed from his preadolescent pores. "You daydream too much. Way too much."

I glanced around, embarrassed. "That's none of your business." Whew, it sure seemed like I was saying or thinking those words a lot these days.

Phil must've picked up on my aggravated state. He dropped the fanciful reverie remark and opened my algebra book. "Let's begin, shall we?"

"Oh, puh-leeze, can we just cut the intellectual jazz and talk like normal human beings?"

"Normal? According to whom?"

I shook my head. This was hopeless. "Just explain the stupid homework."

He explained it twice. Then a third time. "Do you get it *now*?"

"I think so."

"Okay, do the problem," he said. "I'll watch."

I worked the problem, slowly . . . carefully.

Then he checked it. "Almost," he said.

"Are you kidding? It's still not right?"

Patiently, he showed me that I'd added instead of multiplying one of the sets of numbers.

I gripped my pencil. "Do you think I'll ever get this stuff?"

Again, Phil pushed up his glasses. This time,

without commenting ... and we started over on another problem.

That's how things went on Tuesday afternoon. Along about an hour into an exasperating tutoring session, Andie had the gall to show up all smiles. With Billy, no less.

"Hey, girl." She came up and hugged me like she hadn't seen me all day. "How *are* you?"

"Okay." No way was I going to elaborate. If she'd had any brights at all, she could've sniffed out the tension between Phil and me.

Instead, Andie surveyed Phil, then the scraps of crumpled-up papers where I'd tried (and failed) to finish the problems. "Oh, I get it. You two are working here," she remarked.

"It's a tutoring session," Phil said.

"I see . . ." Andie was carrying on like she'd had no idea we'd be here. Like this had been some chance meeting. I despised the charade.

Phil spoke up. "We're really very busy now, so if you'll—"

"Assertive little soul." Andie grinned at Phil. "Spunky, too."

For a second I thought she was going to rumple his hair. "Uh, Andie, can we talk later, maybe?" Truth was, I never wanted to talk to her again. Not the way she was pulling this ridiculous stunt. She knew Phil and I were going to be studying here. She *knew*. Why was she acting like this?

Andie turned to Billy. "I guess they're tied up," she said. "But you could give her a call later. Okay with you, Holly?"

A call? About what? About the thing, whatever it was, that Billy wanted to talk to me about at the Soda Straw?

I looked at Billy. "Was this your idea?"

He shook his head back and forth. "Well, kinda . . . I guess."

"So in other words, *no*. Right?" I glared at Andie.

"Shh!" a group of students shushed us. Then the librarian came stalking over.

Phil sized up the situation. "Better beat it," he said to Andie and Billy.

"We'll be quiet," Andie whispered to the librarian when she motioned for her and Billy to skedaddle. Andie pulled out a chair and Billy followed suit. She pulled the algebra book her way, and when I grabbed it to intercept, she clutched it with all her might. "Let me just see it," she demanded through clenched teeth. "Billy knows this stuff. He can help Holly understand . . ."

Phil seized the book, too. "Excuse me? This is *my* responsibility."

Andie looked at Billy, as though giving him the cue to jump in. She waited, looking as if she might blow up. Billy, on the other hand, said nothing.

Then it hit me. I knew why she'd come. Billy was just supposed to waltz in here with her and take charge—show me he could tutor me just as well as, if not better than, Phil. Andie, in her delusional state, hoped that Billy and I would hit it off as tutor and student . . . then discover we liked each other. Maybe a lot. Of course that's what she'd planned. I would bet my cat on it!

Andie held on to the book for dear life. "Philip Patterson, did anyone ever tell you you're a nerdy kid?"

Phil wasn't going to let academic slurs stop him. "If the textbook splits, you'll have to purchase a new one," he stated matter-of-factly.

"That's the least of my worries," she hissed.

Suddenly Phil let go.

The book—along with Andie—went flying, knocking down one of the chairs and a stack of library books behind her. "What a little brat," she said, getting up.

I'd had it. "You . . . you are despicable!" I'd never meant something so much in my life. "How dare you talk to my . . . my. . . ." For a second I didn't know what to call him.

But I recovered quickly. "Phil's not only my brousin; he's my friend. Now go, before *I* kick you out."

Phil's eyes nearly popped out. I'd defended him— to his face!

Andie glared, and Billy seemed a little disoriented. He'd never heard such words fly from my sweet lips. In fact, right now if I could have, I would've dreamed up a far-flung future for myself. Away from Dressel Hills, Colorado. And Andie, too.

16

As if things weren't already bad enough, they instantly got worse. Andie flew out of the library. Billy, however, stayed seated and calmly surveyed the stormy situation.

Until . . . in walked Paula Miller. Talk about awkward. This was it.

My hunch was she would ignore us, pretend she hadn't seen Billy sitting across the study table from me.

But I was wrong.

She came right over, "Well, hello," she said, taking Billy into consideration as she spoke.

I was speechless. Billy wasn't. For pretty much the first time since he'd walked into the library, he spoke. "Have a seat."

Paula pulled out a chair next to me. Her perfume was sweet, like she'd just sprayed it on. "What's everyone studying?" she asked.

Phil took the opportunity to take her small talk

literally and began rehashing my algebra homework. He continued while I glanced nervously at Billy, who seemed to be taking the situation in stride.

Paula, however, was sending me signals with her eyes, as well as poking me under the table. It seemed like she was tapping out a code of some kind on my knee. Something like: You promised. You promised. . . . Of course I couldn't be sure, but it certainly seemed to fit the rhythm of the words.

When Phil finished his spiel, Billy seemed convinced that my brousin was the best tutor for me. Paula, however, didn't show any interest in that. She was seething under the table, but her face never showed it.

"I think it's time we head home," I said, making the first move to call this nightmare meeting adjourned. Phil started gathering up the papers. And while he went to dump the balls of wadded paper in the trash, I said good-bye to Billy, who was in an obvious rush to get going.

Paula and I stood there for a moment, waiting until Billy disappeared down the stairs and out the front door. Then she cut loose. "I thought we had a, well, an understanding."

"We do, or rather . . . we did."

"Then why are you and Billy here—together?"

"I'd hate for you to think I'm making this up as I go, but I had nothing to do with Billy showing up. Just ask Andie."

"Andie?"

Phil came back and picked up the algebra book. "Ready?"

"Almost," I said. "Meet me out front." I turned to Paula. "Andie's having some trouble sorting out reality—"

"Why is it," Paula interrupted, "that you constantly blame Andie for your own errors?"

I noticed the librarian creeping up, so we scurried to the door. Once outside, it wasn't as easy to talk. Phil was waiting.

"I'll call you later, okay?" I offered.

"That won't change the fact that your word is definitely mud." Paula walked away, holding her head high. I hadn't seen her so perturbed since our seventh-grade feuding days. That, too, had been a tiff over a guy.

"Well," I said to Phil, "I guess it's time we catch the bus home."

We walked almost a whole block before he said anything. "You caught me off guard earlier."

"Oh?" I could sense what was coming.

"You called me your friend. It was quite shocking."

I poked him in the ribs playfully. "Don't let it go to your egghead, tutor-boy!"

♥ ♥ ♥

At home I got busy on my English assignment. I had the perfect idea. I wrote the title at the top of my paper: *If Only I Could Know the Unknown Future.* Wow, this sort of an essay would knock the socks off

Mrs. Ross. Maybe I could weave some sci-fi lingo into it. Phil could help with that.

My first draft was rougher than usual. It had something to do with thinking constantly about the weird scene in the library this afternoon. I couldn't believe things had gotten so crazy. Made me wonder if Andie and I were through for good. The way I felt right now, she didn't deserve a friend like me.

Paula Miller didn't, either. She hadn't given me the benefit of the doubt, the way I would have if the tables were turned. Paula had behaved true to form—pounding away at my knee and maintaining a calm, cool face, though her searing eyes made it clear she was rattled.

And Billy? He acted really strange around Andie. Totally unlike himself. I felt sorry for him. Andie had obviously railroaded him into going to the library with her. Whether or not he knew I'd be there was another story.

One thing was sure: Phil and I had experienced a moment of truth. Straight out of nowhere, I'd stuck up for him. Now I knew firsthand what the saying meant—"blood is thicker than water."

Coming to this conclusion—and actually experiencing such a thing—would've been enough for one day. But, as it turned out, the phone rang after supper, and Billy was on the line.

"Hello?" I said.

"Hey, Holly. Thought I'd give you a quick call."

"Yeah?"

"Getting right to the point . . ."

Whatever that is.

"Paula called me earlier," he said. "She told me you were asking around about my handwriting. What it looks like, to be exact. So . . . what's this about?"

What had Paula said to him?

In a flash, I knew. This was her way of getting back. I'd messed up the deal with her, so she'd broken her promise to me about not telling Billy about the weird letter I'd shown her today. Some friend she was.

"Uh, Holly? You still there?"

"What did Paula tell you?"

He mumbled like he wasn't really sure what she'd said or why she'd called. I could relate to his feelings about it. After all, some people *I* knew could come across rather fuzzy on occasion, especially when they were upset.

"I really think it's probably just a big misunderstanding," I said.

"Huh?"

I almost let myself think, *Poor Billy, stuck in the middle.* But I wasn't going to do that. Billy, after all, was as cool a guy as there was in Dressel Hills. Probably one of the coolest. But, of course, he was no match for Sean. And even as I talked to Billy, trying to smooth over the ridiculous situation at hand, I was thinking of Sean Hamilton. Of strolling along a palm-scattered beach with him . . . out in California. Where I really wanted to be.

"Holly? Did you hear what I said?" Billy asked.

"I'm sorry. I've got a lot on my mind."

"Hey, don't worry about it. Probably nothing important anyway."

I agreed.

"Well, I'll see ya."

"Okay," I said, forgetting that he'd wanted to meet me at the Soda Straw "to talk" a few hours earlier. After we'd hung up, I remembered.

Just now, our conversation had been a total flop. My fault. Maybe Phil was right—I *did* daydream too much.

Funny how a person could go from one extreme to the other about a brainy brousin. All in a single day.

After a warm bath, I sorted through the latest stack of letters to *Dear Holly* and found Paula's letter. I had stopped to check my personal editorial cubbyhole before heading off to the library. Now it was time to catch up on some correspondence.

I opened the envelope and read Paula's note, cleverly written. But she had used such big words, and I really couldn't see the point of her letter. She was congratulating me on acquiring assistant editorial status for *The Summit.*

Thinking back to what had transpired between us earlier, I wondered if Paula might now be wishing she hadn't written this at all. Fact was, I'd solved one major problem—the strained relationship between Phil and me—rather spontaneously. But in doing so, I'd created two more problems. How could things get so complicated this quickly?

I patted my bed and Goofey jumped up, purring as he found a warm spot next to me. Opening my devotional book, I discovered that the Scripture for October 22—today—was 2 Corinthians 12:9—"My grace is sufficient for you, for my power is made perfect in weakness." It was the second time this verse had come to my attention this week. So . . . was God trying to tell me something?

For a moment I wondered if Uncle Jack had borrowed my teen devotional book for the family's time together the other night. But, no, I knew better. He would've asked permission.

I read the "Think it Through" section, contemplating my weakness (my anger and big mouth, in this case). I thought, too, of how God's grace could make me strong. But there was a catch. I needed to ask. Plain and simple. *Ask.*

I had been waiting for grace to rain down on me. As I read more of the devotional, I realized that God's grace was with me, in me—because I belonged to Jesus. What I hadn't realized before was that I needed to ask the Lord for help with my impulsive nature.

I got out of bed and knelt down. Goofey stayed put, listening in on my prayer. "Dear Lord," I began, "I'm grateful that your power is strongest when I'm weak. I know *you* know how weak I was today. Please forgive me for mouthing off to Andie and Paula and for losing my cool, too. I'll try harder next time. Your grace is enough, and I thank you for it. In Jesus' name, amen."

Getting up, I knew I'd settled some important things spiritually. I just wished I didn't have to learn things the hard way. Now . . . how to get Andie and

Paula to believe me when I apologized?

♥   ♥   ♥

Two days passed, and neither Andie nor Paula would let me get close enough to atone for my sins. Oh, I tried, all right. But they were ticked. Could I blame them?

Billy offered a solution when he and I ran into each other at lunch. "Tomorrow, first thing, Andie has student council. Why don't you try to talk to her then?" His face didn't flush red while we talked this time. Something was different.

"Did Andie say anything to you . . . about, you know, the thing at the library?" I asked.

"She only said she couldn't believe you'd thrown a fit like that." He blinked twice, looking at me. "By the way, about that talk we were going to have. When do you want to meet me?"

"Maybe we'd better skip it. If that's okay with you."

"Cool." He leaned against the locker next to mine. Like he was beginning to relax around me. Like the old days before all this bizarre infatuation started.

"To tell you the truth, I'm a little confused. I still get the feeling that Paula likes you. Did you two actually split up?"

He rolled his eyes. "That's another subject."

"Really?" I was dying to hear it from Billy's lips.

"I better not try to explain now." He looked me straight in the eye. "And I hope you and I won't become enemies over this."

"Over what?"

He blushed then. "Well, you know . . ."

So I was right. Billy still liked Paula a lot, even though he seemed to be struggling with some sort of feelings for me. Yet I was sure everything would work out for the best in the end.

♥ ♥ ♥

Friday, before school, I planted myself in front of the student council office door and waited for Andie. I wanted to make amends. Desperately wanted to.

Five long minutes had come and gone when Ryan Davis showed up. "Hey," he said, smiling.

"Looking for someone?" I asked, although I figured it was Zye Greene.

He stuck his hands into his pockets. "Waiting for the man. You?"

"Andie."

"Cool."

Then Jared came over, all smiles. I hoped he wouldn't mistake my cheery reaction to his being there. Actually, he was the "out" I needed. Truth was, Ryan totally bugged me. In the past, his obvious prejudice toward Andie—toward all dark-skinned people—had made me furious. A sort of righteous anger. Of course, I didn't hate him or anything. But

I certainly couldn't stand his half-flirty, half-witted comments here lately.

Jared stood so close I could feel his shirt sleeve against my arm. "How's the most popular editor in the school?"

"Guess again."

"C'mon, Holly-Heart, you'll be terrific," Jared gushed.

"We'll see." I was thinking about that ridiculous reply I'd written to "Who Am I?"'s letter.

"When's the paper coming out?" Ryan asked.

"Monday."

Ryan's face lit up like the Fourth of July. "Great!"

"What are *you* so excited about?" Jared asked Ryan, who was still hovering near me.

"I think I'm going to be published—at last," Ryan said.

Jared shrugged like it was no big deal. "Wouldn't be the first time Mrs. Ross twisted someone's arm to write an article for the paper."

I could see these two guys weren't crazy about sharing the same turf with me. And I was relieved when the office door opened and Andie walked out. "Hey, girl," I said, scurrying down the hall after her. "I need to talk to you."

She kept walking, not talking.

"Look, I'm trying to apologize."

Andie huffed. "I saw fire in your eyes, Meredith." She was referring to Tuesday afternoon. The day she and Phil were fighting over *my* algebra book.

"You looked absolutely hateful." She scowled.

"Do you really dislike me so much? You caused a major scene!" She headed for the girls' room and darted in. Before I could get to her, she disappeared into one of the stalls.

"So what does it take to say 'I'm sorry'?" I asked, standing with my nose to her door.

Silence.

"C'mon, Andie, we can talk this out . . . we're best friends."

"*Were.*"

I stood my ground. "Please, can't we just talk?"

"You already said that, but you know what? I think you should just forget about Billy Hill and get yourself grown up a whole lot and then go off to college and maybe marry your fine and fancy Sean Hamilton and get as far away from Dressel Hills as possible." She sucked air into her lungs.

"Okay, now that that's off your chest, are you finished?"

Tomblike silence.

"Andie?"

"Leave me alone," she fired back.

So I did. I checked my hair in the mirror and walked right out of the rest room.

But feelings of rejection overwhelmed me, and I almost didn't see Zye and Ryan on the opposite side of the hall. When Ryan's eyes finally caught mine, I snapped to it, hurrying down the hall past them.

"Holly-Heart." He rushed to catch up.

Shocked that he'd used my nickname, I whirled around. "Don't ever call me that."

"But it's your name, right?"

"Not exactly." I turned away from him, longing for the safety of my locker. If only I could get away from this obnoxious person. If only . . .

Just then I spied something pink and heart-shaped stuck to my locker door. "Oh, great," I muttered. "What's this?"

"Looks like someone's got a secret admirer," Ryan said, still following me.

I stopped cold in the middle of the busy hallway. "Excuse me! I don't know what you want, but if you don't mind, I'd like to be left alone."

He grinned. "Sorry there, Holly, just wanted to clear up one thing." He glanced down the hall. "Uh . . . back there, when your friend Jared said something about Mrs. Ross asking me to write an article for *The Summit*—well, she didn't ask me, nothin' like that. Okay?"

I was completely unprepared for his totally foggy account. "Whatever." I said it just to get him out of my hair.

Surprisingly, it worked. Ryan turned and headed the other way.

Quickly, I got to my locker and snatched off the . . . *valentine?* What on earth was this for?

I opened it and read the verse:

> *Roses are red,*
> *Andie is blue,*
> *I think it would help a lot*
> *If she stayed away from you!*

No signature. And besides that, the poem had been printed, not written in cursive. I studied it carefully. Nothing to go on. I glanced around the hall, hoping for a clue. This mystery-letters-and-notes thing was really getting out of hand. I wracked my brain all the way through first and second hour and was still obsessing about it in algebra.

Bravely I showed the valentine note to Jared, who was sitting behind me again, oddly enough. He read it and handed it back. "Sounds like you and Andie really tore into things."

"That's not why I showed you this," I insisted. "Does the *printing* look familiar to you?"

He shook his head. "Nobody I know prints like that, but if you want my opinion, I think some girl probably sent it."

"Thanks for nothing." I turned around in time to see Mrs. Franklin staring at me. Looking down at my desk, I was embarrassed. What would she say about my homework today?

"Holly, may I see you after class, please?" she said.

I nodded without looking up, worried sick about another F grade, or worse—flunking algebra altogether. Not worried enough, though. Because, as hard as I tried, I could not keep my mind on the new assignment. I figured Phil would say I'd done it all wrong anyway when I got home, so why waste my time trying?

Instead of doing algebra problems, I doodled. Even concocted another scene for my novella, which had begun to suffer due to lack of time. My powers of concentration were focused on tutoring sessions. That, and worrying about the friends I was losing because of my bad temper.

And there were the mystery letters and now an anonymous valentine poem. Who was writing them? And why?

18

Mrs. Franklin's face showed zero emotion as I sat next to her desk. The classroom was empty, and she and I were alone again, just the two of us. I tried to bolster my bruised ego.

Glancing at my watch, I knew I'd probably be late for fourth hour. Mrs. Franklin would be more than willing to write an excuse for me, though, and probably include the reason for my tardiness on top of it.

I waited as she opened her desk drawer and found a file folder. "Here we are." She looked at me momentarily. Her face seemed almost relaxed, instead of pinched up. Was this going to be good news after all?

I was puzzled.

"Holly, your stepbrother is doing an excellent job, I do believe."

"He is?" I squeaked.

Was this a backhanded compliment? I couldn't be sure.

She pointed to my score for our last homework assignment. "You missed only five problems."

Five out of thirty.

"This is definitely an improvement," she said. "Now, I want you to continue working with Philip for another week or so. We'll see how you're doing then."

I nodded. "Thank you." I wasn't sure why I said that. Maybe because she had intimidated me so much before today. Anyway, I felt encouraged. And more confident than I had in two full days.

After lunch I waited for Paula at her locker. She and her twin were strolling down the hall toward me. They stopped talking immediately when they saw me.

"Is this your idea of funny?" I held out the valentine to show them.

Paula sauntered to her locker, flicking through her combination. "Andie and I have had it with you, Holly," came her words. "For someone who's going to be answering letters to the editor, and—"she paused, glancing at Kayla—"and for a Christian, well, you are certainly not reflecting God's grace to the school population."

God's grace. There it was again.

I nodded. "I agree with you, Paula, and I'm here to say I'm sorry about Tuesday." I waited. She said nothing, so I continued. "I just want an answer about this valentine poem," I said, "and then I'll be on my way."

"Holly, you can't just walk away like that." This time Kayla was doing the talking.

"I'm not trying to avoid either of you. I just think that right now Paula may not be interested in patching things up." I sighed. "By the way, have either of you met any perfect Christians?"

Paula's mouth dropped. "Well, I . . . I, we try to follow the Lord's example in all things."

I smiled. "Don't most Christians? But notice, you said *try*, and trying is exactly what I'm doing. Tuesday, I failed. Big time. But if apologizing and trying my best to stay cool by walking away from a potential hot spot offends you, then, once again, I apologize."

I turned to go.

"Wait," Paula said.

Surprised, I froze in place. Kayla's brown eyes twinkled.

Then Paula confessed. "I wrote that stupid poem. I think we, Andie and I, went a little overboard, though."

Smiling, I was delighted with the way things were turning out.

Paula ran her hand through her hair. "I accept your apology, Holly. Now"—she pointed to the valentine—"will you forgive me for that?"

"Gladly."

The Miller twins smiled matching smiles as they resumed their chattering.

I hurried down the hall, wondering if the same approach might work on Andie. The more I thought about it, the more I knew she would reject me even more if I came across too boldly.

How could I get to her without stirring up more

anger? Should I have someone else, another friend, tell Andie how sorry I was? I figured Jared would be more than happy to fill the bill. And there was always Billy. Paula, too. But I wanted to handle this mess myself. After all, I'd started it. So I needed to finish it . . . with God's grace.

Leaning against the wall, I wondered how I could ever get Andie to listen to me again.

Then it hit me. I knew exactly what to do. Right after school I would start working on my plan. In fact, I would start the minute I got home.

However, there was the usual pressure from my tutor to get to work on the algebra homework I'd brought home.

"Give me one hour," I told him. "Then I'll be ready."

Phil grinned mischievously and set the timer on his watch. "Sixty minutes it is."

I ran to my room, pulled out a pen, and began to write:

Dear Andie (On behalf of the "Dear Holly" column)—

I know it's too late to get this published in the school paper this month, but could you see that Holly gets it for me anyway?

I just had to write. You see, I have this best friend—I won't mention any names—but believe me, she's been my best friend since we were toddlers.

Anyway, my friend and I got into this horrible fight the other day. Actually, she wasn't all that bad. I was the one who ended up saying the really horrible things. (I'm sure if my friend reads this, she'll know what I'm talking about!)

I want you to help me tell her that I'm sorry (honestly sorry) without making her mad, because right now—actually, for several days—she hasn't wanted to have anything to do with me. Sure, I've tried to talk to her, but she's still ticked. And I don't blame her. Nobody should be called despicable. Nobody!

I really need your advice.

Signed: A Best Friend (I hope!)

I read what I'd written. This type of letter was my best shot, a little tricky, but it might work. I hoped so. Later on this weekend I would take time to revise it. But in the meantime, I'd be praying for Andie, that her heart would soften toward me. That she wouldn't view this attempt as stupid.

Stroking Goofey's fur, I thought how clever it would be to print out this letter using one of the cool fonts on my computer.

"Your hour is up," Phil called from downstairs. "Tutor time."

"I'll be right there," I called back.

Quickly, I concealed all evidence of the letter. Then I headed downstairs.

Phil was extra patient this session, not that he hadn't been all week. I did notice that something had changed between us. He was nicer. And not as greasy-haired.

Maybe I was trying not to zero in on his negative aspects so much. Yeah, maybe that was it.

Anyway, Phil explained each of the new problems. Then he worked some of his own homework while I did my thing. Looking over at him, I remembered what Mrs. Franklin had said about Phil. "Hey, guess what my teacher told me today?"

He scratched his head. "Something about your work?"

"Nope, something about *you*."

He pushed up his glasses. "Me?"

"She said you were doing an excellent job."

A crooked smile crossed his lips. "Which means, you're catching on," he said, bouncing the compliment back to me.

"I think you're right." I leaned back in my chair. "I think I'm finally getting it."

"It helps when you have a friend for a tutor, right?"

I laughed. Phil would probably never forget what I'd said last Tuesday. That was okay. Things had worked out between us. Far better than I'd ever dreamed possible.

Mom strolled through the dining room. "Well, well, looks like the master and student are hitting it off."

I twirled my pencil, grinning at Phil.

"Maybe Holly could tutor Carrie," Mom said. "She's been having lots of trouble with long division."

I groaned.

"Might as well pass on the knowledge." Mom headed off to the kitchen.

"Pass it on," I said softly, going back to my algebra but thinking more about what I'd learned from the verse in 2 Corinthians. Maybe I'd share it with Andie. Once we got over the current hurdle and were speaking to each other again, that is.

Only time would tell. Next Monday, to be exact.

Saturday a letter showed up in the mail. The mystery writer strikes again!

I scanned the page, nearly bursting with laughter. This time I was being asked the ultimate personal question. (Not will you marry me?—but close.)

Dear Holly,

Because you are a sweet, kind person, I thought you wouldn't mind if I sent this to your home address. Although you have not answered any of my previous letters, I have high hopes that you might choose one of my letters for your "Dear Holly" column. Am I on the right track, thinking this way?

Perhaps you are wondering about me? (WHO is he? WHAT's his problem? WHEN will he ask me out? WHY is he writing all these letters? WHERE will it all end?) Well, that takes care of the 5 Ws. Now, do you think it's strange—the things I write?

Spare me—this was too much!

> *From what I've heard of your work, you are a talented writer, possibly headed for greatness. HOW do I know this?*
>
> *I pay attention when Mrs. Ross happens to be name-dropping in class. I enjoy her literature classes a lot. And I also like hearing about one of her star students. You!*

Hmm . . . literature with Mrs. Ross. Interesting. This guy's definitely an upperclassman, I decided.

> *I hope you will meet me for a long, get-better-acquainted chat. The pen-and-paper method is getting old. I'm hoping to have a better idea of how you feel about me on Monday when I read your column—that is, IF you selected my letter to be published.*
>
> *Another secret admirer,*
> *WHO am I?*

Thank goodness, there was no P.S. this time. Shoot, the main body of the letter was filled with enough nutty things to fill a fruitcake. Yet I tried to fit the puzzle pieces together as I reread the letter.

Then something hit me. Those words: *Another secret admirer.*

They were like an echo in my brain. Sometime this week . . . in school . . . in the hallway . . . somewhere very recently, someone had referred to the pink valentine note as coming from a secret admirer. Who was it?

Think, I told myself. *Think!*

Then it came to me. I swallowed hard, trying not to choke on the realization. Could the person who'd said those words be the same one who had written them?

Yikes! I freaked out in front of my cat. And Goofey arched his back in protest.

Wait a minute. This guy said he wanted to meet me in person. Just then, a sense of relief came over me as I realized, thankfully, the weird writer could *not* be Ryan Davis. After all, I'd already met him— several times.

♥   ♥   ♥

Sunday was a real disaster.

Andie wouldn't even let me sit with her in Sunday school. The Miller twins were aghast. So was Jared. She got up and moved when I squeezed through her row toward the vacant seat next to her. Our teacher raised her eyebrows but probably assumed it was just a mere adolescent struggle. Mere, of course, by no means described Andie's rage.

I sat down alone and soon was surrounded by Paula and Kayla. "I wouldn't be surprised if Andie's totally embarrassed next week at this time," Kayla offered.

Her comment didn't make me feel any better. Andie, however, needed time to chill out. Unfortunately, I assumed her time was up for such nonsense. Counting today, which of course hadn't completely transpired yet, it had already been five days since the library fiasco. Hadn't I been punished enough? But I would not lose my cool and tell her so. Nope, my letter to her would have to suffice. Tomorrow!

During class I caught Billy watching me. And there sat Jared—girlfriendless. What an unusual turn of events. Amy-Liz, however, didn't seem upset by it, even though she'd done the dumping. She was sitting between Joy and Shauna near the front of the class. Jared's eyes weren't on Amy-Liz, though. They were twinkling at guess who. Would this boy ever grow up?

Danny Myers, on the other hand, was way too mature for his own good. Any girls who were even remotely interested decided to play it cool when they found out how serious and severe he was. Kayla Miller included.

Stan, of course, didn't count. He was just a brousin and not so proud of it. Funny, I'd thought last November, before Mom and Uncle Jack married, that Stan and I might be close stepsiblings some day, but when it came right down to it, Phil was the one who'd won my heart. Phil and little Stephie—when she wasn't snooping in my room.

So that was pretty much the extent of the guys my age. Like I'd told Andie last week, there was no future for me here in Dressel Hills. At least, no romantic future. But as upset as that comment had made Andie, it was positively true. Sean was still absolutely it in my opinion.

Then I wondered . . . could Andie's behavior be an outgrowth of two things? My angry words to her and my stubbornness about Sean Hamilton and his letters?

I wanted to turn around and look at her. Study her face, see how she was sitting. Arms crossed, a scowl . . . what?

Usually my best friend was an open book. Today, however, I couldn't read her so well, probably because she was directly behind me. Tomorrow, though, I would be watching her. Very closely. Somehow, I must see her expression when she read my mystery letter to her.

And what a kick it would be if I could observe the "Who Am I?" guy when he saw his words in print. That was impossible, though, because I had no idea who he was.

20

It was unusual for Stan to ride the bus to school. But Monday morning, my oldest brousin surprised me and walked to the bus stop, even sat with me.

"What's the occasion?" I asked.

"Can't a guy ride to school with his little sis?"

"Little? I'm almost as tall as you."

He shrugged. "Well, you know."

"No other reason?" I was fishing. But Stan was no dummy. He knew.

"Okay, so today's kinda special," he admitted. "You're a celebrity, right? Everyone's going to be reading the latest feature column in the school paper. Who knows? Your name might become a household word."

"Maybe . . . if students like what they read."

He glanced at me. "Having second thoughts?"

"It's just that some weirdo is writing personal stuff to me." I told him about the mystery letters.

"Any clues who's sending them?" he asked.

"At first, I wondered if it was that guy you hung around with last summer. Ryan Davis?"

Stan laughed. "Why would Ryan want to write you anonymous letters?"

"Well, he *does* want to be published. *The Summit* would be an easy way, maybe."

Stan ran his fingers through his blond hair. "Still, I can't believe he'd stoop to something like that."

"There's more," I said. "The mystery writer wants to have a long talk with me. He said he was tired of the pen-and-paper method of communicating."

"Ryan's never been shy before. I doubt he'd say something like that."

"Have you ever read any of his stories?" I asked.

"A few."

"Any good?"

Stan shifted his books. "For one thing, he writes a lot different than he talks."

"Well, believe it or not, Marcia actually liked the first letter I got from the weirdo and decided to run it, along with my crazy response. So if it *is* Ryan's letter, he ought to be pleased."

When we pulled up in front of the high school, Stan was still thinking out loud. "Hey, wait a minute!" He stood up, holding on to the seat. "Come to think of it, Ryan was asking questions about you."

"Really?" I got out of my seat. "When?"

"About two weeks ago, I think."

"Well, that's when the letters first started."

Stan looked surprised. "You sure?"

"Positive. How could I forget? I mean—those letters—they were so freaky."

Stan headed for the front of the bus. I followed. Then, I couldn't believe it—he actually walked me up the steps and into the school. Definitely a first.

Even Billy Hill noticed. Jared, too.

"So where're you headed?" Stan asked as we took our time weaving in and out of students.

"English, of course. I'm dying to see how my column looks."

"Okay, I'll see you later." Stan stopped and waved. "Good luck, or break a leg, or whatever."

I chuckled. Why was Stan going overboard being so nice to me? And what did he know about Ryan that he wasn't telling?

I dashed into the English classroom, which doubled as the newspaper office. Mrs. Ross and several other students were counting out papers for the various homerooms.

I had seen the layouts before they'd gone to press but not the final copies. Eagerly I pulled a paper off the stack and opened to the third page—prominent right side.

There it was—"DEAR HOLLY." The first column of my entire life. The heading was snazzy, printed in a stylish font—almost a literary-romantic look. I scanned the whole thing, rereading the mystery letter, which was followed by my reply.

"Man, if this *is* Ryan's letter, I'm doomed," I blurted out. I could see it now. I'd be the laughingstock of the upperclassmen. Not that I cared; it was just so humiliating.

So how could I know Ryan was the culprit for sure? Should I confront him? Would he even admit it?

Mrs. Ross was peeking over my shoulder. "Holly? You look upset. You should be pleased. You've done a marvelous job. I had to laugh out loud at the interesting letter from that mysterious writer."

"I'm glad you liked it." I closed the paper. "Everyone did a fabulous job. And thanks for your help, too, Mrs. Ross."

Marcia Greene and several others who'd written articles came up to congratulate me. I thanked them and volunteered to take *The Summit* around to the senior class homerooms.

Perfect. I would drop the papers off in the various classrooms and hang around when I came to Ryan's homeroom—while he read the paper. If he carried on and showed everyone the letter, I would know I'd solved the mystery. If not, I was back to square one.

There was only one problem with my plan. I had no idea whose homeroom Ryan Davis happened to be in. Maybe Stan knew, so I scurried down the hall to his locker.

When I got in the vicinity of his locker, I realized that Stan had already gone. Rats! Who else would know?

I stopped in the middle of a swarm of kids to wrack my brain. Then I knew who to ask. Marcia Greene's brother, Zye, was good friends with Ryan. Surely Marcia would know something.

I made a beeline back to Mrs. Ross's classroom, still carrying the pile of newspapers.

"Marcia just left," Mrs. Ross said when I inquired. She eyed the stack of papers in my arms. "I thought you'd gone to deliver those."

"I was, but . . ." No time for explanations. "Guess I better get going," I said over my shoulder.

"Better hurry—there's a pep rally for homecoming first thing after homeroom this morning," she reminded me.

I'd forgotten. If I didn't hurry, I wouldn't get a chance to observe Ryan Davis reading the paper. Then all this thinking and planning would be for nothing.

Instead of trying to track down Marcia or her brother, I headed straight for the school office. The secretary would know about such things as homeroom locations. Perfect.

I raced upstairs, lugging the papers. Too many kids were crowding the stairwell. Still hurrying, I tripped on the next to the top step. The papers flew down, scattering every which way.

A few polite boys stopped to help, but when the bell rang for homeroom, I found myself quite alone. Out of breath and racing against time, I scurried around like a frantic little mouse gathering up the loose papers. If I hadn't had a specific mission—a serious goal—this scenario would've seemed almost funny.

At last, I restacked the papers and trudged back up the steps. So much for celebrity status. Stan was wrong. I was actually a lowly freshman peon. Shoot, I couldn't even deliver papers.

Frustrated, I marched, huffing and puffing toward

a designated homeroom. I didn't even knock, just headed in and placed the papers on one of the student's desks and left.

The plan I'd concocted involved standing outside each of the senior homerooms and peering in inconspicuously, searching for Ryan, hoping to observe his expression. Unfortunately, I couldn't find him anywhere. I craned my neck back and forth, trying to spot him at each classroom.

He simply wasn't there.

Discouraged, I dashed down the hall to the stairs and headed back to English. "I need an excuse for class," I said to Mrs. Ross, who was sitting prim and proper at her desk. "I had a little accident with the newspapers, and now I'm late."

She smiled, disregarding her homeroom students, and pulled out the appropriate form, filled it out, and signed her name. Then, before I left, she mentioned something about a guy bringing me a letter. "I believe it might be from a secret admirer," she said with a smile.

Mrs. Ross pulled out the top desk drawer. "Here you are, dear." Some of the kids in her homeroom snickered.

"Thanks." I ignored the whispers flying around me, feeling my suspicions rise. My curiosity won out, as always, and I opened the envelope as I hurried to my locker.

Dear Holly,
    Congratulations! You must be totally jazzed about your new column. I know I am (happy for you).

This sure didn't sound anything like the mystery writer. I read on.

> I'd like to work things out between us, Holly-Heart. Remember last year, before things changed so radically? Think back. . . .
> Please, won't you give me another chance? I promise I won't mess things up this time.
>
> > Always and forever,
> > Your #1 Secret Admirer.

This letter was no mystery—it was from Jared Wilkins. Had to be!

> P.S. By the way, I heard about those letters you've been getting. Paula said she read one of them, and she's right; they're NOT from Billy. If you want to know who wrote them, meet me in front of the cafeteria. I'll be the one smiling.

Why, you. . . ! I thought. Jared would do anything to get my undivided attention—even pretend to have information on the mystery writer. What a rat. But would I fall for yet another master-minded plot from the master of flirtation himself?

I was about to mentally nix the idea as ridiculous when, just as I rounded the corner—within a few yards of my homeroom—Ryan Davis appeared. "Holly, you're just the person I've been looking for."

"I am?"

"You did a grand job of putting together that column of yours. Even Zye was impressed. He's the senior class president, you know."

"Yeah, I know." I looked around to see the pep

squad coming toward us. "Are you headed for the assembly?"

"I'm in charge of the sound system."

"Oh." I kept waiting for him to mention his letter in the column. "Did you get a chance to read *The Summit* yet?"

"Sure did. It's great. You have a way with words."

"Hey, thanks." I glanced toward Mr. Irving's classroom. "I'm late for homeroom. Better get going."

"See ya." He turned to go.

"Thanks again." *Thank heavens, you're not the mystery writer,* I thought as he left.

I hurried to my homeroom, and several kids clapped when I stepped foot into the room. "Three cheers for Holly!" Mr. Irving said in French.

I gave him my signed form and then hurried to my desk, my face turning red.

"Holly," Mr. Irving was talking above the noise of the students. "We're all wondering about that interesting letter in your column. Will you tell us who wrote it?"

"Oh—the 'Who Am I?' guy?" I replied. "Well, I'm sure no one will believe this, Mr. Irving, but I honestly don't know."

Groans came from around the room. Even Amy-Liz looked disappointed. And Jared? Well, I refused to look in his direction. Nope, Jared had pulled another fast one. And for all I knew, *he'd* written the stupid letters.

21

After the pep rally I headed for the girls' room.

Paula and Kayla were redoing their hair in front of the mirrors, helping each other like sisters do. "Holly, hey," Kayla said, looking over at me.

"What an exceptionally good column," Paula cheered. "Accolades to the writer."

"Thanks." I plopped my backpack on the ledge below the mirror.

Paula stopped brushing her twin's hair and strolled over and started fooling with mine. "Did you ever find out who wrote that strange letter?"

"I really thought I had this mess figured out, but I honestly have no idea," I said. "Any thoughts from either of you?"

Kayla shook her head.

I pulled out the latest letter. "This one is not a mystery to me. It's got Jared's name all over it."

Paula and Kayla surrounded me, reading it. In seconds, both girls were laughing. "What'll we do with that boy?" Kayla said.

"That's what I want to know. Do you think he might know who's writing letters to me?"

"You could take the chance and show up at lunchtime and find out," Kayla suggested.

Paula grinned. "But Holly doesn't want to get anything started again with Jared, right?"

"Who would?" Kayla scoffed. "He's lonely for one reason—because Amy-Liz got wise to what he's about."

"But what if he's truly changed?" Paula asked. She'd always had a soft spot in her heart for the guy.

Kayla commented, "How is that possible?"

"People do change sometimes," Paula replied.

I looked at her reflection in the mirror. "You're kidding, I hope."

Paula smirked back.

"Andie says you've got a guy friend in California," Kayla said. "Does that mean Dressel Hills boys are out of the picture?"

"For now," I replied.

Paula whipped out a mini bottle of hair spray. "Surely you wouldn't pass up a chance to go out with some of Colorado's most dashing males. Remember, you'll be fifteen soon."

"In February," I reminded her. "Mom says I can go on a real date then."

"You'll snub *our* guys here?" Paula asked.

"Surely you won't abandon them," Kayla echoed.

I frowned. "You two sound like Andie. Did she put you up to this?"

A mischievous expression crossed Paula's face.

I shook my head. "Andie's gotten to you, hasn't she?"

Kayla touched her soft curls. "Gotten to me?"

"Yeah, because Andie's after me to dump Sean. She has her reasons. Pretty pathetic if you ask me."

"That's interesting." Paula put away the hair spray.

I laughed. "C'mon, you guys. I know you've already had this conversation with Andie. She's filled you in on her latest goal. Sounds like paranoia, but you know how Andie is sometimes."

They nodded.

"No matter what she or anyone else says, I'm hanging tough on Sean. He's so cool you wouldn't believe it." The three of us headed for the door.

"Well, to give up a chance with Jared, he certainly must be extra special," Paula said, trying to be serious. That's when I chased her down the hall.

❤ ❤ ❤

After government class I rushed to Andie's locker. I wanted to deliver my own version of mystery—the letter I'd written Friday night. I smashed the envelope into the air vent of her locker and skittered away.

Down the hall, I stood behind an open door, holding the school paper open in front of me, hiding. I felt the muscles in my shoulders tense as I waited. How would Andie react to my letter?

And, then . . . there she was. Andie headed straight to her locker and opened it with a jerk. My letter was waiting at the bottom of her messy locker. She leaned over and picked it up, her face scrunched into a bewildered look.

Watching her like a hawk, I peered around the paper as she stood reading my letter.

I held my breath.

What would happen? Would she crumple it up . . . toss it away?

Then, surprise, surprise. Andie did a strange thing. She called out to me. Called my name loudly. "I know you're watching from somewhere, Holly. Get yourself over here, girl!"

"What on earth?" I muttered to myself. And go, I did.

"You silly," she said, hugging me. "What sort of letter is this?"

"A nutty one."

"You can say that again." She was giggling. When she calmed down, Andie said she was sorry, too. "I shouldn't have called your stepbrazen a brat."

"*Brousin*," I said.

"Huh?"

"Forget it; I get the idea." I laughed.

"So how's the tutoring going?"

I used her skinny locker mirror to primp. "I'm actually learning some math, finally."

Then a peculiar look crossed her face. "And, uh . . . how're things with Sean?"

"We correspond pretty often. Why?"

"Just wondered." I turned to look at her. Now

she had a squirrelly sort of grin. "Guess I've been a jerk about that, too."

"That's okay."

"What a waste of emotional energy," she admitted. "Even if we do go separate ways in the future, we'll always keep in touch, right—no matter what?"

"Always."

She closed her door and hoisted her books over to her left arm. "Uh-oh." She stared down the hall. "Guess who . . ."

I turned to see Zye Greene and Ryan Davis.

"It's the Double-X Files," she muttered.

"Aliens at school?" We laughed.

"Something like that," she whispered. "Hey, did you hear? Ryan might be coming to our church youth group."

"You're kidding. Really?"

"Danny Myers invited him. Danny is trying to evangelize the entire Dressel Hills population, I think."

"That's good, isn't it?" Suddenly I felt sick inside. I'd treated Ryan poorly. Just because I didn't agree with his racial prejudice was no reason to reject him as a person. A person who was most likely struggling like the rest of us—probably searching for truth. Bold Danny had the right idea whether Andie approved of it or not.

Now Ryan and Zye were coming our way.

"I wonder what they want," I said.

"Well, I'm outta here," Andie said, turning to leave. "I'm not hanging around to find out."

I stood there for a minute. It was time I stopped

being so rude to these guys. Sure they were upper-classmen, and yep, they'd humiliated Andie and me during freshman initiation, but they were human beings. Jesus had come to save them, too.

Zye stopped a few yards away to talk to another guy, and Ryan spotted Stan, who was fumbling around at his locker. The two of them stood there talking like old friends. Once, Stan glanced over at me, looking a little sheepish.

I headed for second hour, wondering what was going on. Were Ryan and Stan hanging out again? And if so, why hadn't Stan told me this morning on the bus? Things were absolutely confusing.

During choir Andie and I sat together for the a cappella songs. We were forming a unified front against Jared Wilkins, who kept looking my way, try-ing to get my attention. By the time class started, I'd filled Andie in on his mystery note.

"Don't do it," she strongly urged. "Do *not* meet him for lunch. He doesn't know a thing; I can almost guarantee it."

"Paula says we can't be sure," I teased.

Andie opened the music folder, ignoring my comment. "There has to be a better way, you know, to find out who's been writing those letters."

"Will you help me?"

"Super sleuths to the rescue!" she said, laughing. Knowing she had agreed to join forces with me made the solving all the more intriguing. We would get to the bottom of all this. One way or another!

In algebra class Mrs. Franklin passed our homework back to us. I did a double take on mine. There was a big, red A, almost the way a grade school teacher would write it, high on the top of my paper. I'd missed only one problem.

After class I showed Andie. "Check it out."

"Well, congratulations. The girl not only writes, she does math," she joked.

We were headed down the hall when I noticed Ryan. He was standing in front of my locker, blocking it.

Andie took charge. "Excuse us, please!"

Ryan didn't budge. He was looking at me like he wanted to talk.

"Oh, I get it," Andie said. "You want some privacy." She backed away, and Ryan smiled.

"Hey, wait up," I called to her. Then, slowly turning, I looked at Ryan. "Mind if I open my locker?"

He stepped aside. "You know," he began, "I think you should keep writing . . . a lot. You're very good."

"Thanks." I thought he'd already said that earlier.

"Everyone's talking about that one letter, uh, that mystery dude."

I reached for my English notebook. "Yeah." I laughed. "Even my homeroom teacher asked me about it."

"So, like . . . who is it? Do you know?"

"Beats me. But I intend to find out."

Ryan scratched his chin. "I bet I know someone who could help you with that."

I shut my locker. "Who?"

Ryan ran his fingers through his mousy brown hair. "You're lookin' at him."

"You?"

"Hey," he said, holding up his hands. "It started out as a joke—Zye's idea. But the more I thought about it, the more I liked it. Writing secret letters to a pretty editor. A real kick."

I still couldn't believe it. "Stan told me there was no way it was you."

His eyebrows arched. "He said that?"

"Not exactly, but—"

"Well, Stan was the one who helped set it up," he blurted. "He gave me your home address and all."

"He did what?"

Ryan nodded. "Someone else helped, too. Someone who says he and you were close friends once."

"Don't tell me. Jared?"

"Looks like you've got at least two guys paying close attention these days." He started walking with me.

Sean's the only one who really matters, I thought.

"You're not mad, are you? I mean, it's not so bad, is it, getting letters like that—from a secret admirer?"

I refused to lead him on. Wouldn't be fair. And by his smile and the way it looked like he was going to walk me all the way to fourth-hour class, it seemed as though he liked me, too.

Ryan began to explain. "For the past few weeks, I've wished I could do something to change your mind about me. I was a bigoted jerk about your friend Andie. Nobody can help who their parents are. Or their skin color."

Was he apologizing for his prejudice?

He kept talking. "Another one of your friends has been talking to me about going to church. We've even discussed the creation of man and how we're each made in the image of God. Wow, that struck me as real cool."

My mind was still reeling. "Danny knows what he's talking about."

"You got that right. The guy knows the Bible upside down . . . inside out." Ryan's eyes were shining. "Danny knows something else, too."

I didn't need to ask. It probably had something to do with Danny and me—how we'd gone together way back in seventh grade.

"I'll say this," Ryan continued, "whoever the guy in California is—the dude you're writing to—well, he should be counting his blessings. 'Cause the guys back home are feeling shut out."

"That's nice of you," I replied, deciding not to tell him it was none of his business about Sean.

Out of the corner of my eye, I saw Jared and Stan hanging back, trying not to be seen. I turned and waved, and they fled.

I wanted to finish my conversation with Ryan before encountering the likes of either my brousin or my former first crush.

"More than anything," I said, leveling with Ryan, "I'm glad you said what you did before about racial hatred. It's a frightful, destructive thing, not only for the victim, but also for the person doing the hating. I'm glad you've had a change of heart, Ryan."

The bell rang.

"You're quite a girl," Ryan said. He turned to leave.

Something in me wanted to tell him I would actually miss reading his creatively weird letters. But I watched him go in silence.

I wondered, as I took my seat in my next class, if I, too, had been prejudiced. Thinking back, I realized I'd sized up Ryan based on my emotions at the time. Shoot, I'd tuned him out last summer because of a pimple.

Sure, he'd shown despicable signs of racial prejudice, but what had I done to help him? It had never crossed my mind that I should invite him to church or have a serious talk with him about God's plan for mankind.

I had messed up.

♥ ♥ ♥

I met Jared before lunch. After quickly filling him in, telling him I already knew who my mystery writer was, I excused myself and went to the library. There, I found a quiet place. Alone.

Without being noticed, I pulled my tiny New Testament out of my backpack and found 2 Corinthians 12:9: "My grace is sufficient for you, for my power is made perfect in weakness."

Thank you, Lord, I prayed from my heart. *Thanks for your grace. Please help me always remember what Ryan said today. Show me how I can help others. Not just my Christian friends, but others, too. Amen.*

I pulled out my spiral notebook and began writing to Sean Hamilton. He was anxious to hear about the success of my column. I'd have to remember to scan a copy of *The Summit* to email to him.

And there was something else very important, too. I wanted to share the Bible verse in Corinthians with him—the one that had made all the difference for me.

About the Author

On her twelfth birthday, Beverly received a book titled *As the Day Begins*. It was the devotional that helped her through her junior high years and beyond. "I read and reread that book," she recalls. "It was one of the best birthday gifts ever."

Beverly still has the devotional book. It shares a bookshelf with many favorites from her youth. Sometimes, when she's feeling like a kid inside— "Which is a lot of the time," she admits—Beverly will curl up and reread familiar passages.

About getting mystery letters . . . occasionally, a reader will write to Beverly at her Web site, eager for a reply. But if no return email address is included, it is impossible for the author to answer.

Happy reading!

You can write to Beverly by going to *www. BeverlyLewis.com*. Be sure to include your email address!

Also by Beverly Lewis

The Beverly Lewis Amish Heritage Cookbook

PICTURE BOOKS

Cows in the House • *Annika's Secret Wish*
Just Like Mama • *What Is Heaven Like?*

THE CUL-DE-SAC KIDS
Children's Fiction

The Double Dabble Surprise	*Tarantula Toes*
The Chicken Pox Panic	*Green Gravy*
The Crazy Christmas Angel Mystery	*Backyard Bandit Mystery*
No Grown-ups Allowed	*Tree House Trouble*
Frog Power	*The Creepy Sleep-Over*
The Mystery of Case D. Luc	*The Great TV Turn-Off*
The Stinky Sneakers Mystery	*Piggy Party*
Pickle Pizza	*The Granny Game*
Mailbox Mania	*Mystery Mutt*
The Mudhole Mystery	*Big Bad Beans*
Fiddlesticks	*The Upside-Down Day*
The Crabby Cat Caper	*The Midnight Mystery*

ABRAM'S DAUGHTERS
Adult Fiction

The Covenant • *The Betrayal* • *The Sacrifice*
The Prodigal • *The Revelation*

ANNIE'S PEOPLE
Adult Fiction

The Preacher's Daughter • *The Englisher* • *The Brethren*

THE HERITAGE OF LANCASTER COUNTY
Adult Fiction

The Shunning • *The Confession* • *The Reckoning*

OTHER ADULT FICTION

The Postcard • *The Crossroad*
The Redemption of Sarah Cain
October Song • *Sanctuary** • *The Sunroom*

www.BeverlyLewis.com

*with David Lewis

Just for Girls!

Answering Questions From Girls Like You!

Sandra Byrd loves interacting with girls like you who read her books. In fact, she gets letters all the time and has developed a series of books that address the questions asked to her most often.

In *Girl Talk* Sandra covers issues like school, family, faith, and friends, and also includes fun quizzes and questionnaires.

In *The Inside-Out Beauty Book* Sandra looks at health, beauty, and how not to lose focus on staying beautiful inside.

Join the fun and see what girls like you across the country are talking about!

A Winning Series About Fun and Friends!

Sandra Byrd's HIDDEN DIARY series follows two new friends who have found an antique diary whose pages will lead them on countless adventures and mysteries. Join along and treasure both the friendship as well as the timeless, godly messages in each book.

1. Cross My Heart
2. Make a Wish
3. Just between Friends
4. Take a Bow
5. Pass It On
6. Change of Heart
7. Take a Chance
8. One Plus One